Wolves in white collars

Wolves in white collars

Roger Wheatley

For Tom

The author lives in Canberra, Australia, with his wife and family.

Prologue

"Reckon we'll die here?"

The shooting had stopped. The two men sat in the dust, shotguns across their legs, backs to the rear wheel of the ute, out of sight of the men across the clearing.

"Let's not be overly pessimistic," said his friend.

Before either of them could say anything further, someone yelled to them. The two men looked at each other. They knew that voice.

1

It was an awkward moment, not the kind that might make an onlooker wince, but it was somewhere in the vicinity.

Luny hadn't meant for his jibe about his friend's coffee-drinking ritual to come out with such vigour, but there it was, like their coffees, on the table.

He'd witnessed it hundreds of times, his friend letting his coffee sit for an eternity before drinking it, spouting some wanker rubbish—as Luny called it when he ribbed him—about letting the meniscus thicken.

But today's comment had an edge to it. They both sensed it. His friend looked at him from across the table, his coffee untouched in front of him.

He responded, his words clipped. "I believe I am

paying for this coffee, Luny, and if I choose to let it sit here, staring at it until ice forms, then that is my prerogative." Dek's mouth was half its normal width.

"Sorry," said Luny, after a brief pause. "Bad week."

Dek looked at his friend and nodded almost imperceptibly, accepting the olive branch.

They were both relieved. Their Saturday morning schedule was back on track. It was important for both of them.

And it was a great day, the spring sun was out, there was no breeze, and having scored the perfect table, leaning back in his chair, Luny shifted his focus to enjoy the uninterrupted views of passing foot traffic.

Dek ordered smashed avocado, poached eggs, goats cheese, dukkah and wood-smoked bacon, raising an eyebrow when Luny asked for raisin toast.

"Where's the big breakfast, the sausage, the mushrooms? Watching our figure are we?"

"Something like that," replied Luny, offering nothing further. The truth of the matter was that Luny had already eaten bacon and eggs at Stella's house. But knowing that any reference to Stella—particularly one that impacted the Saturday brunch routine—would not be well received, he kept it to himself.

"So how's the new super agency?" asked Luny, in an effort to shift the focus away from what he was eating and why he was eating it. He knew Dek would take the bait, his workplace having recently been amalgamated with another government department. Dek was not happy about it.

"You have no idea. That fucking biartch I work for is a walking advertisement for how shit it all is. She's like a shark circling me, watching every little thing I do. I need to get out. I'm never going to get promoted when they're cutting jobs and nepotism is rife. But of course, there won't be any jobs anywhere. Every other department is in the same position. I'd love to just quit, but I couldn't pay my mortgage."

"So, not much change then?" Luny added.

"Hmm," was all Dek added to the matter, "and what about your bad week."

Luny worked in IT. The work was not taxing, he would say with a smirk, that was the responsibility of the Tax Department.

"Same as last week. No staff, shit systems, and a constant stream of whinging clients. Toppo, you might say. Unfortunately I can't find the energy to give a big enough shit to do something about it."

"A malaise."

"A malaise indeed."

"What are we going to do about it?"

"Same as ever, nothing."

Dek pushed his plate back, the knife and fork neatly together—looking like they were in a relationship—at six-thirty on the plate. He dabbed at the corners of his mouth with the smallest portion of napkin, and then placed the napkin, folded, on his plate. He looked his friend in the eye.

"This won't do you know. We're two bright and capable chaps, in a bit of a rut. We need to find an out. We're better than this. We're educated, we're experienced. The world is our oyster."

"We're shit-kicking middle management, with no real skills, other than dealing with arse-holes on a daily basis. Apart from another public service job, who's going to want us?"

"Come on Luny. Lateral thought, we need to think outside the square here."

Both men sat without saying anything for a time. Luny broke the silence.

"How about crime. That's outside the square."

"To what end? How is this going to repair our miserable existence, take us forward?"

"How about retirement? That's taking us forward. And what about just doing something interesting and a bit dangerous?"

"Well, that'd certainly take care of my mortgage issues one way or another. We'd either be rich or, if the crime went south, I'd be getting free board and food, courtesy of the Australian Government, in some high security prison."

"Yeah, but all the sex you want…or didn't want."

"Very droll. So what did you have in mind?"

Luny sat forward in his chair, a little more animated.

"Something big, just once. I watched *the Inside Man* again last night. I love that flick. If we do something it needs to have panache. We won't be running through the front door waving guns around. No, I'm more your tunnel-into-the-vault kind of guy."

"Although, laundering cash troubles me," Luny said, screwing up his face, looking pained. "Have you ever thought about it? If you had a huge stack of stolen cash what would you do with it?"

"Spend it of course, go nuts," said Dek.

"Therein, as the Bard would tell us, lies the rub."

"Lies the what, says who, what are you on?"

Luny shook his head in mock dismay.

"It's a line from *the Inside Man*. The movie actually misquotes it, which most people do. It's from Hamlet. The Hamlet line actually says, 'ah, there's the rub', but people most often say 'therein lies the rub'."

Dek stared at his friend in disbelief.

"How is that we're friends?"

"I was going to explain about what you said about spending the money we steal. You said, you'd go nuts spending it, and I said, 'therein lies the rub', which means that's where the problem is."

"I know what it means Luny. What are you telling me?"

"Look, the downfall of many a stupid criminal—present company excluded of course—is brought about by doing what you said you'd do. If you rush out and start splashing cash all over town, people will notice."

"Think about it," Luny went on. "You couldn't pay off your flat, or even buy a new car. Government spooks are watching for changed spending patterns. You suddenly whack two hundred grand in the bank to pay off your loan and someone will be knocking on your door in short shrift."

"You're not making this sound like a winning proposition," Dek was getting bored.

"No, no, don't be discouraged, it'd be fine, we'd just have to be sensible. I've thought about it. You simply keep the money somewhere secure, like in a safe somewhere in your house, and you just use it for day-to-day living. There's lots of stuff you could use it for, just very carefully."

"Well, I'll bear your sage advice in mind when I find myself in possession of a large wodge of unexplained cash…ever mindful of the rub."

"Well, it's the getting-bit we need to focus on," said Luny. "The spending bit is a problem I'm sure we'd like to have."

"Well, you focus on the getting bit and I'll go off and do my shopping. Good luck with it."

Dek dropped a twenty on the table and left Luny staring off into space.

While Dek did his shopping, Luny headed to the comic store to pick up the latest edition of *Prophet*. A text from the store owner—Luny was a valued and long-time customer—earlier in the morning, alerting Luny to the arrival of his current favourite tome, had been most welcome.

Luny had a large collection of comics. He freely admitted it was the only area of his life where he was as fastidious about cleanliness and order, as Dek. He'd been keeping his comics from an early age and such was the size of his collection, that the bulk of them were stored in his old bedroom at his mother's house.

The comic store was his cave. The plastic wrapped

volumes were his porn. It was way more than the stories. The smell of a new comic tantalised his senses. The crisp scent of clean, unsullied paper and ink he found heady. The two shiny staples in the spine set against the primary colours of the content pleased his eye.

Sometimes he worried that he might be pigeon-holed with the other sad fuckers who prowled the aisles. The store really was a confluence of the weird, but harmless. He had explained to Dek that he rarely engaged in conversation with anyone other than the owner.

The owner nodded a silent greeting in Luny's direction when he saw Luny enter the store. Far from being perturbed by Luny's abrupt demeanour, the store owner welcomed the opportunity to avoid some ridiculous, hour-long discussion on the merits of various super powers. As far as the owner was concerned, Luny was more than welcome.

That night, after Dek had fed his mum, seen her off, and cleaned up the kitchen, he sat down to watch the news on his white leather couch, stretching out with a glass of Pinot gris.

Dek liked nice things. He glanced around the room, content with what he saw. His home was tasteful and neat, the way he saw himself. He fancied himself as a bit of a clothes horse, having once let slip during a drunken evening with Luny and others that he thought he looked a bit like Val Kilmer in *Top Gun*, perhaps a little taller and slimmer. The addition of aviator-style sunglasses in daylight hours was no coincidence.

While Luny would never say a word about Dek's self-appraisal, he did think the hairstyle and outfits were a shade too young for Dek's years. Luny wondered what the male version of mutton was called.

Dek's home was all too nice for Luny's taste. *Villa Olde Farte* was how he described it, often asking Dek when his safety rails and panic buttons were going to be installed. Luny sneered at the twee green-space and bench seat in the middle of the complex. He accused Dek of dragging down the age average from eighty five.

Dek didn't care what Luny thought. But what he did care about was his disposable income, and more to the point, how little of it there was after his monthly mortgage repayment. He should really take in a boarder. He knew that, had thought about it many times. But he always reached the same conclusion, he couldn't bear the thought of someone touching his things, or worse, fouling up the bathroom.

He really wanted a promotion. He need a promotion. But he wasn't thinking of this when the news started. He was relaxed and not thinking of much at all other than the ripe tropical fruit notes of his wine, when the first item caught his attention.

The newsreader crossed to a reporter standing in front of a police car on a Canberra suburban street, *"Shots were fired today into this Canberra home behind me. Police are investigating leads into bikie-related gang warfare, and the growing drug crisis on Canberra streets. Police investigators have asked for any witnesses to come forward with any information."*

Dek frowned.

2

The next week promised to be a busy one for Dek, as he prepared for an event with the new government minister. This was Dek's bread-and-butter, and he quite enjoyed the detail of putting a launch together. But what he didn't enjoy, and didn't need, was someone looking over his shoulder.

Although he probably shouldn't have left the office in this busy week, Dek figured a few minutes with Luny would be beneficial to both him and his work.

"She's been circling me like a shark," were his first words to Luny, as they sat at an outside table at the cafe they frequented on work days.

"We're two days out from the launch and do you know what is causing us the most grief? Oh, it's not a questionable policy commitment by the government, no, it's that the cloths on the morning-tea table at the launch don't match the floral arrangements!"

"But it doesn't stop there. No, there's also the major problem of the lectern sign being too wide for the lectern—did you even know that they made lecterns of varying widths?"

"This is my world," Dek went on. "Honours degree, and ten years of government experience and I'm spending the morning on the phone going between the fucking caterer, the fucking florist and the fucking venue manager. It's so depressing," said Dek clamping his teeth each time he uttered the word 'fucking'.

It wasn't often that Luny could match Dek's tirades but this morning he had something up his sleeve.

"My dip-shit supervisor took me to a meeting with a branch head this morning," grumbled Luny, his chin in his hands. "It was a fucking ambush, he had all of his directors there. And you know why?" Throwing his hands in the air, he sucked in a breath. "To fucking complain about the IT service they weren't getting. Numb-nuts walked us straight into it. He just sat there and took twenty minutes of heat over something that isn't our fault. God it's depressing."

"On a brighter note," said Dek. "I've solved your

problem about who we should," Dek glanced around to see if anyone was nearby, leaning closer to his friend, "steal from. One word. Bikies."

"What, steal their bikes? You planning to set up a Harley stall at a Sunday trash 'n' treasure between the pre-loved books and the aromatic candles."

"No, not the bikes. Their money, you idiot. I watched it on the news last night. Bikie gangs are fighting over drug turf in Canberra. They're the ones you see getting around town in their filthy jackets with the logos on the back. And don't get me started on those bikes.

"How do they get away with making so much noise in a public place?" Dek spat with venom. "It astounds me. If I had a faulty tail-light on my car, I guarantee you, that a cop would pull me over and hand me a fine within the day. And yet, these tools... these neanderthals, ride around making noise loud enough to rupture an ear drum, and no-one troubles them."

"Calm yourself old chap or you'll pop a valve," soothed Luny.

"How do the cops let them get away with it?"

"Probably scared of them," said Luny. "Like any sensible person."

"But that's who we should steal from," said Dek,

"not a bank. Bikies are all criminals, selling drugs, running brothels, protection rackets, they must have heaps of cash. That's *who* we should rob. It would take the cops out of the equation. The bikies would never report the crime. And it really wouldn't be stealing. It's money they've made illegally. It'd be a victimless crime."

Luny snorted.

"Oh, there'd be a victim alright. The headline in the paper would read, '*Canberra man victim of bikie torture*'."

"A Canberra public servant," Luny continued in his newsreader voice, "was found today by police, hanging from a meat hook with his testicles severed and jammed into his mouth. Neighbours recalled muffled screams and a foul stench coming from the man's apartment earlier in the day."

"Very funny, but hey, as you said, only if they catch us."

"What's this 'us' business, kemosabe? You're on your own with bikie gangs, I'll stick to tunnelling into vaults thanks very much."

Dek looked at his watch.

"Gotta go, the shark will be wondering where I am. We'll talk more about his later."

"No we won't," said Luny to Dek's departing back.

Stella. That was Luny's biggest problem. Not work, or IT crap, or even Dek's obsessive behaviours. It was his relationship with Stella.

She flummoxed him.

Without needing the constant reminders that others provided, Luny knew, that Stella was way out of his league. She was hot, and smart and on the way up, already a branch head, even though she was a couple of years younger than Luny. This didn't bother him at all, what concerned him—as it seemed to worry so many others—was what she saw in him.

Luny was a slob. He knew that. The word fashion did not have a big role in his vocabulary. The crutch of his jeans hung low, revealing a stomach-turning view of hirsute arse-crack at inopportune moments. And he was hairy. A pelt of red fuzz covered large tracts of his ample frame, front and back, giving rise to the "Wookie" moniker afforded him during his university days. His close-cropped red hair—*number-three-all-over-thanks-barber*—grew in tufts. Like feuding Scottish clans, each cluster doing its best to avoid contact with its near neighbour.

What Luny didn't bother to explain to others was that he had no control over the relationship, was no part of its instigation or its management. He basically did as he was told.

It was Stella who approached him at the departmental Christmas party over a year ago. No-one was more surprised than Luny.

Given he could barely string a coherent sentence together in her presence at the time, he was gobsmacked when he found himself having a dinner-for-two at her house that night. He had loosened up fractionally after waking up in her bed the next morning.

Luny's dating history was checkered at best. There'd been a couple of drunken flings at university, and a three-month relationship with a single mother he'd met at work. When she had told him that she had reconciled with her husband Luny was very relieved.

But he was sure he didn't want to spend the rest of his life alone.

The thought of prowling the aisles of the comic store—Luny had a passion for comics—into his fifties, looking for someone to speak to, left an unease in his guts that was hard to shift. But he felt only slightly less uncomfortable about his relationship with Stella. He really had no idea what was happening, so he followed his usual plan of action, the path of least resistance.

There was no predictability to the relationship. Some weeks, he would spend several nights at her house—she never stayed at his place, having a similar view to Dek's about his living standards—but then he might not see her for several weeks. There was rarely any explanation for this. He simply answered the phone when it rang and did as he was bid.

Dek hated Stella. He hated her because she was in senior management and several years younger than he, he hated her because her rise would continue, he hated her because she dressed strangely, but most of all, he hated her because she had him figured out within two minutes of their first meeting.

Luny had invited Stella to Saturday brunch with Dek, just once. It had been the most excruciating forty-two minutes of torture. Under her scrutiny, Dek's replies got shorter as Stella's probing questions got longer. Dek had not even waited for his second coffee, before bolting to the warm bosom of the supermarket.

There had been one brief reference to the event between Dek and Luny, just enough to ensure that such a calamity could never occur again. Stella's only reference to the event was to ask Luny if Dek was gay. It wasn't the first time someone had put this question to Luny.

Early on in their friendship he assumed Dek was gay but now he wasn't so sure. There had been no men or women in Dek's life, beyond some friendships, in the time Luny had known him. Either way it didn't matter to Luny.

3

"Well, I survived another shark attack," said Dek the following Saturday, leaning back into his chair after finishing his baked eggs with Spanish tomato sugo, chorizo and tapenade.

"The event went very well, as they always do. The minister was very happy and gave us all a nice pat on the head. It's just ridiculous the amount of time, effort and angst that it takes for thirty minutes of toss. The shark was beaming and at her vomitous best. You would think that she was the most relaxed person in the world the way she flits and flaunces around these events."

"I'm not sure flaunce is a word," was Luny's contribution.

"Well it should be, it's what she does," replied Dek,

dismissively. "God I hate it. She even told me how nice the flowers looked on the tables. I hope it comes up at Government Estimates." Laughing he said, "I'd love to feed a question to one of the Senators and have the Secretary invite the Shark to answer it."

Leaning in closer to maintain Luny's full attention, Dek found his rhythm, "could you please tell me," said Dek in a voice of much gravitas, "how many people, and how much time and money was involved in putting together the floral arrangements and the table cloths at the recent launch?" Slapping his knee to emphasise his point, "that I would like to see."

Before Luny had a chance to say anything further, the conversation was interrupted by a noise so loud that conversation was impossible. Like many of the other customers, the two men turned to see three Harley-Davidson motorcycles and the sneering, fuck-off, countenances of their riders hanging from high bars, rumble past the cafe. Dek beamed as they rode away.

"It's a sign Luny."

"What?"

"The bikes."

"Righhhhhht?

"Those were Harleys. And we're going to rob them."

"On the strength of being annoyed briefly over brunch, you intend busting a cap in their arses. I shall be keen to add this to my list of first-world problems," said Luny laughing.

Angry eyes flashed at him as Dek held a finger to his lips, "Shh! No, no-one needs to be shot, we'll just rob them of a large stack of money. And it's not on the strength of five bikies riding up the street. It's on the strength of spicing up a boring existence, for both of us."

"Dek old son, you need a good lie down."

"No, I'm serious."

"And so am I. You keep planning, and I'll keep living in the real world," he said pushing up from his seat. "I've got to go, I have to go to some lunch with Stella and I need to get changed."

Dek's farewell was a brief roll of the eyes but he said nothing further, even though he was very keen to point out that Luny had only just finished eating eggs Benedict with smoked salmon.

"There seems to be two main bikie gangs in Canberra, Satan's Mongrels, and the Ferals," said Dek during a mid-morning coffee break the following Monday.

He had spent quite a bit of time on the Internet on Sunday researching and taking notes.

Firstly, he had reasoned, they would have to work out whom to steal from—he smirked to himself when he kept writing 'we', knowing full well that Luny would have to be his partner in any such ludicrous adventure. And that was another point; it had to be a crime that could be carried out with just the two of them. There would be no way he would involve anyone else.

Bikie-related activity in Canberra had spiked in the media of late so it wasn't hard for Dek to find a long list of recent references. In previous weeks shots had been fired at a couple of suburban houses, these activities police had suggested were turf-related between different bikie gangs. While it might not be Milperra, Dek came to realise that Canberra was not immune to the problems of the real world.

The thing that jumped out at Dek from the media reporting was that every police raid seemed to net three key items: drugs, weapons and cash.

"There's been a bit of argy bargy between them of late, shots fired and people wounded, that sort of stuff," Dek continued. "I reckon we'd have to start by targeting these two clubs."

"Two points I'd make at this juncture," his friend

interrupted with a raised hand. "Firstly, are you still thinking about this crazy shit? Secondly, have a listen to yourself, they're shooting at each other. What would they do to you? You'll notice the final word of the previous sentence was 'you' meaning stay the fuck away from me with this idea."

"No, no," said Dek, "Hear me out. The shooting is good news. It means there must be something worth fighting over, and it has to be drug territory and that means, drug buying and selling, and that means—what do you call it—fat wads."

"The term is fat stacks," Luny was a big fan of *Breaking Bad,* and proudly sported a Heisenberg t-shirt among his collection of bad-taste regalia. "But fuck fat stacks, they'll kill YOU, very slowly."

"Luny, listen. The beauty of us stealing from them is they would never be expecting it. They would blame the other gang. No one would ever think of looking at a couple of boring public servants. We just need to be smart about it."

"Smart is saying, no fucking way! I can't believe that you're actually sounding serious about this?"

"I must say my rotund chum, I am a little surprised to hear you speak in this mousey, squeaky, voiced way," prodded Dek.

"You're nuts, you know nothing about them,

nothing about whether they even have cash, and certainly nothing about where said money is going to be, and when. Nuts, nuts, fucking nuts."

"We research and plan. We can do this. We're the perfect criminals. No history, no connections. No one will ever know. Just once, and then we can cruise with some serious cash."

"Ok, ok. Just say we managed to do it—and I'm not saying we do it, it's fucking crazy—but what would we do with the money. How do we launder it?"

Dek noted that it was the first time Luny had said 'we' when referring to the crime.

"I've thought about what you've said, when you go on about drilling into bank vaults. We'd keep it simple. Keep it at home and only use it for living expenses, no big purchases just day-to-day things. That's all we'd need."

"The spooks and those Tax pricks keep an eye out for people whose living patterns suddenly change," Luny said, his voice serious.

"I reckon we'd both be smart about it, I don't think it's a problem," said Dek.

"Alright, so say we go ahead—and I'm not saying I will, but if I did—what's the next step?"

"We need to find out if they have drug buys or something like that. We need information. I've thought about this. I reckon the simplest way is to bug them."

"Whaaaaat!"

"Luny, you surprise me. Look, I've got to get back. I've got a meeting. I'll drop over tonight. I've got a few ideas."

They lived not far apart but that's where the similarities ended. Where Dek's apartment was light and airy and tastefully furnished, Luny's was a festy hovel—words employed by Dek to describe it.

Dek description of Luny's living arrangements were never destined to be favourable when the first thing he had to do on arrival at Luny's building was to struggle up five flights of stairs to the top floor, muttering about the absence of a lift.

Luny had stripped out his bedsit apartment to bare walls and rebuilt it to his liking. It was painted midnight blue—the name he fired back at Dek when Dek dare suggest it was black. It was a model of efficiency and function, as Luny was fond of explaining. His kitchen, just inside the door, consisted of a small bar fridge complete with a glass door, a two-burner stove with griller—Luny loved toasties—and a small sink. His limited range of eating and cooking utensils were stored on a shelf over the sink next to his microwave.

A translucent glass screen partially concealed his shower and toilet in the back corner of the room.

His pride and joy was his bed, which was fixed at a height against the wall to enable a shortish person to walk under without bumping his or her head. Underneath Luny had set up a desk and his computing equipment.

A massive, very old, brown, leather couch—a bequeath from Luny's grandmother— dominated the final corner of the room. It and a recliner rocker were positioned facing a ninety inch television which occupied most of the wall.

The television was Luny's most recent purchase and had cost him close to twenty thousand dollars, and he loved it. In between the couch and the screen a glass-topped coffee table held an assortment of gaming DVDs, movies, a Play Station and an X-Box. In relation to the two gaming consoles, Luny subscribed to the view that in different games each machine had its advantages over the other.

Dek found the door to Luny's apartment unlocked. This never ceased to annoy him. Given the look of some of the building's tenants, he thought Luny very careless. Luny didn't look up when Dek entered, engrossed in qualifying for a race on the Nurburgring.

"Won't be a sec," said Luny. "Ah, there we are, front row of the grid." Luny saved his position and paused the game.

"Can you turn it off," said Dek, referring to the ninety inch screen showing Luny's car in pause mode, "it freaks me out."

Luny flicked the television off and turned to his friend who had sunk into the rocker.

"Righto, tell me how we're going to die."

"Alright, here it is. We need to bug their club," as he said this Dek held up his hand, forestalling any response that Luny was about to launch in his direction.

"I've done a bit of research and we can buy a bug off the Internet for not much over five hundred dollars that we can put under the floor of their club. It has a range of several hundred metres so we don't have to be too close to the club. The trick is getting it in there."

"Get in where, who are we bugging? You're fucking nuts."

"We go with the *Satan's Mongrels* to start with. They seem to rate the most press coverage in relation to drugs in Canberra. And they've got a club; well it's more of a house, down south. I've driven past it."

Reeling back in surprise, Luny didn't know whether to be shocked at the suggestion of bugging a bikie club or be astounded by Dek's initiative. But any small amount of respect quickly withered as Luny changed tack.

"And you Mr. Practical, you who has trouble using a can opener, are going to crawl under a house teaming with spiders and god knows what else, a house populated by tattooed monsters who would think nothing of shoving a double-barrelled sawn-off shotgun up your arse and pulling the trigger, and put this thing in position. This I have to witness."

"Well, we can discuss who is better suited to which task, but first…"

"No fuckin' way," Luny exploded, "you hear me, ain't no fuckin' way I'm doing this."

"Look, we can talk about it. You said yourself I'm not the most practical of people. But before you get yourself tied in a knot, let's order the equipment."

"Fine, and what are you ordering?"

"I've done a bit of research on the 'net," Dek was pleased to get off the subject of who would be 'installing' the device, knowing he had a better chance of exciting Luny with something electronic and high-tech.

"There's lots of stuff around. I figure we need something that we can switch on and off remotely to reduce the chances of detection if they happen to do scans. It will also prolong the battery life. Log on to this address," Dek handed Luny a yellow post-it, "and have a look at this one I was thinking about."

Tapping his fingers on the arm of the rocker Dek sat quietly for five minutes while Luny ran through the web page.

"That looks fairly sensible, but given I know shit about these things it isn't saying much. Give me a day to do a bit more reading."

"Cool," said Dek, releasing a big breath of air. He had buy-in from his friend.

"This one's over seven hundred bucks. I imagine you're expecting me to go halves with you."

"Given we'll split the cash fifty-fifty it seems fair," Dek's words sounded more like a question than a response.

A noncommittal grunt was all Dek got from Luny.

"Alright, fuck off and let me do some reading," were Luny's last words on the subject.

Dek walked out the door, pulling it closed quietly

behind him, without saying goodbye knowing better than to say anything more at this point.

"This is kind of cool," were Luny's first words when they had a coffee break the next day. They bought takeaways and made sure they were sitting in a quiet spot on a bench well away from any potential eavesdroppers.

"There's a whole world of surveillance options out there and some amazingly slick gear."

This was the kind of response Dek had been hoping for.

"So there's three basic groups of listening devices," continued Luny. "First there are passive devices, which, once installed, require stimulation by a radio signal from outside."

Suppressing a smile, Dek couldn't help but tingle with the rise of excitement he heard in Luny's business-like tone.

"Very sophisticated, and very expensive, and, unlikely that we would be able to purchase one anyway. They seem to be the domain of spy agencies."

"The second group are microphones. They can be hidden almost anywhere. But they require wires and are a little fiddlier to install."

"The third group are units that contain a microphone and a small transmitter, which is what you showed me yesterday. The signal is picked up by a receiver that can be positioned hundreds of metres away from the source. Sadly, I have to agree with your research, I think you've found the best device for our needs. We could go with something more sophisticated and a lot more expensive but I think the set up and installation would be a lot more complicated."

Running a hand across his chin Luny said, "The problem is, I couldn't find anything that showed whether these units would pick up sound clearly through floor boards, but unless you could get a bug into the house, we don't have a lot of options."

"The one you found has the added advantage of being able to be switched off and on remotely which helps avoid detection and saves on the battery." Dek ignored the fact that he had said this to Luny the day before, he was just happy that Luny was in.

"Assuming we monitor it for a few hours at a time I figure the battery will last at least a month or so. I imagine we'll be getting pretty fucking bored by that time if we haven't heard anything."

"So we buy it?" Dek spun to face Luny, eyes

scanning Luny's face looking for any sign that Luny was having a go, teasing him.

"We buy it," said Luny, "And given it's only seven hundred bucks I reckon we just blow it off when we've finished with it and not try to get it back. But how do we buy it?"

"What do you mean?"

"They're fucking illegal to use," said Luny. "I don't think it's illegal to buy one, but I'm not sure. I assume there are people from the spook agencies keeping an eye on this stuff, being ordered on-line."

"I hadn't really thought about that," said Dek, surprised and a little annoyed he hadn't considered this, he felt an edge of anxiety bite him. Could this all disappear after all his planning because he overlooked one small, well, one big thing? "But I'm still prepared to buy it. I'll take the risk," he said with a strength in his words he needed to buffer the point.

"Alright, let's do this thing," said Luny.

4

The device arrived by courier six days later, packed in a neat black case. Dek often had internet-sourced purchases delivered to the mailroom at his work to avoid the hassle of not being home to receive them.

Before he had discovered the work-delivery option he loved to whinge to Luny about the inconvenience of retrieving packages from a depot when he had not been home for the courier delivery. He reasoned it took more time to drive to the warehouse in some out-of-the-way industrial area than it would have done to fly overseas and pick it up directly from the seller.

The work-delivery option had solved his problem, but given the nature of the contents of this most recent package, Dek had thought it might not be prudent to send it there. Instead he had asked his elderly neighbour, a man who rarely left his house, if he wouldn't mind signing for a package. He felt slightly guilty about the potential for an eighty five year old man to end up in prison but not enough guilt to stop him doing it.

'*It's here*', was all Dek put into the text to Luny. Quick to reply, Luny said he would be over straight away.

But on this occasion when Luny arrived, he was all business. With the arrival of the 'device'—the name they both used in relation to the bug—the mood was serious.

"Alright, it's pretty," said Luny, after unpacking all the pieces in the box, "but how can we test it?"

"I've been thinking about that. We need a house that's off the ground with a wooden floor, like the bikies' place. Let's go to Merimbula, and stay at the house."

The house was on the south coast and had been in Dek's family for many years. It had belonged to his grandmother who had died when Dek was thirteen and had been used as a family holiday home by the various branches of the family ever since. Luny had stayed there on a few occasions.

"We can drive down after work tomorrow if you

want, have a few drinks at the club and do it Saturday morning and come home again afterwards, or stay the weekend. No one's using the place."

Dek picked up Luny the next afternoon. It was a given they would drive down to Merimbula in Dek's Honda Euro. Dek could barely stomach a trip to the local shops in Luny's Falcon. On the few occasions where a trip had been necessary, he had sat with his feet up, fearing he would soil whatever kind of fashion footwear he might be sporting on the day, in the knee-deep pool of empty take-away food containers, old pieces of unwashed clothing, and computing equipment.

Dek was sure that if Luny left his car for more than a couple of hours in a public car park the council would have it removed, thinking it had been abandoned.

The drive to Merimbula was pleasant and took about three hours. The area they drove through, as they neared their destination, was the scene of Dek's youth. He had lived in the quaint town of Bega until the age of fifteen when his mother had finally tired of his father's infidelities and moved Dek and his younger brother to Canberra.

They arrived at the house at eight-thirty in the

evening after stopping on the way for a quick hamburger.

The car had barely stopped when Luny demanded they head to the 'Ari' for a beer, using the national vernacular for the local RSL club.

They dropped their bags at the house and headed off with Luny forcing a brisk clip for the short walk to the club. Luny felt more at home in this part of the world than Dek. Luny loved the slower pace and the relaxed vibe and friendliness of the locals, not to mention the easy access to dope. The only drawback, as he saw it, was the limited access to computer retail outlets and comics.

Dek felt he had outgrown the area. Luny called him a snob. Dek preened at the compliment.

The men entered the foyer of the club. As a member Dek completed the entry formalities for his guest. They walked past a new dinghy full of fishing gear parked in the foyer with a big sign advertising an Easter bonanza. Letting his eyes linger on the boat, Luny felt the tug of his childhood, cruising the quiet waters of some lake with his father in search of trout.

It was not holiday time and the club held only a smattering of committed local patrons. The chocolate wheel standing at the edge of the bar area alongside a shopping bag full of used ticket stubs, suggested that an early crowd, in for the Friday night meat raffles and badge draw, had long since departed.

Apart from the quiet murmurings of the few patrons, the only noise came from the poker machines carrying on their evil prattle, enticing patrons to feed their hard-earned into insatiable maws.

At the rear of the lounge area on a raised platform, a young man was packing up a guitar, laptop and sequencer after a couple of hours rolling out quiet, Friday-night covers.

As seems to be a requirement of all clubs, an old man, red of eye and unsteady of gait, propped up one end of the bar. His nose resembled an expensive cheese, blue-veined and full of holes. He had that thousand-yard stare that seemed to take in nothing and everything.

"Let's not get hammered," said Dek. "We need to be fresh to fiddle with the device tomorrow. We should do it early to avoid prying eyes,"

Luny, although disappointed he couldn't cut loose, limited himself to four schooners. For a finishing touch, he ordered a top-shelf, bed-time whisky—which in the case of the RSL club was limited to Johnny Walker Black Label.

Dek woke early the next morning, nervous about testing the device. He was very keen for it to work. He had laid in bed the previous night thinking that should it not function appropriately, he would have an easy way out of the madness he was entertaining. And yet, for some reason he couldn't fathom, he really wanted the device to work. He really needed to do this.

He hadn't really given much thought to the idea of actually robbing bikies, telling himself he would think about that when the time required. For now he would be happy to have a working device and then a plan for getting it under the bikies house.

He woke Luny just after seven-thirty, forcing him out of bed with the promise that they could hit a cafe for brunch once they had determined whether the device would work or not.

Dressed in a new pair of navy blue mechanics overalls, Dek was ready for work. On his feet he wore an expensive pair of leather hiking boots—the top-of-the-line, hike-to-Everest-basecamp kind that Dek had owned for several years and which had summited nothing more than a couple of Canberra's modest hills. He was also sporting a pair of gators.

"You look pretty impervious to almost anything," said Luny through a slitted eye.

"Nothing of an insectual nature is going to climb on my bare skin if I have anything to do with it," he said hurrying to leave the room before Luny had a chance to pull back the covers and reveal his naked form. Dek had been caught before.

Stumbling out to the kitchen, Luny found Dek with the device's various parts laid out on the kitchen table.

"Ok," he said, switching to his tech-man alter ego. "Let's see what this puppy can do."

The men walked out the back door of the house, down the wooden steps and around to the side where a small gate broke the white lattice-work concealing the under-floor area. With Dek's aversion to getting dirty, insects and hurting himself, Luny was secretly impressed with Dek's commitment to be involved with placing and testing the device.

Luny got down on all fours and headed through the gate, carrying the transmitter.

"We don't need to go too far," said Dek. "Let's just aim for the kitchen area."

They struggled forward a couple of metres to where they estimated the kitchen was above them.

"Right, this'll do," said Luny, sitting on his haunches. The device had come with a sticky pad with a peal off cover.

"We'll be lucky if this stick's to the floor boards at all," he said, "we'll need to come up with something better."

Switching the transmitter to the 'on' position Luny pushed it hard against the boards. Holding a hand beneath it, he was pleased when the transmitter stayed in position. Crawling back out to the yard, Dek gave himself a serious pat-down when he was able to stand.

"I can see where this is leading," said Luny watching him. "There's no fucking way you could be trusted to put this thing under their house, is there?"

Feeling rather sheepish, Dek chose not to reply.

"Right," said Luny. "Let's turn the radio on in the kitchen and take the receiver out to the car and see what happens."

With the radio dialled to a local station, which was spewing out details of local weekend sporting events, they climbed into Dek's Honda, which was parked in the driveway of the house.

"Fingers crossed," said Luny as he pushed the on-button on the receiver. He had pre-set the frequency as directed in the instructions. Nothing happened.

"Fuck," muttered Luny.

He tweaked the volume and sensitivity levels and both men jumped in their seats as a blast of music suddenly came out of the receiver. Luny quickly adjusted the volume so they could hear the radio.

"Holy shit," said Luny.

"It works," added Dek.

They sat for a minute or so until a song ended—*Total Eclipse of the Heart* by Bonney Tyler—waiting for the presenter to come on line. When she did, and although it was a little muffled, they were able to make out almost every word she said.

"Holy shit," said Luny again.

"Indeed," agreed Dek.

"Let's see what sort of range we have," said Luny.

Dek started the car, backed out and headed up the street. The signal stayed consistent until they turned the corner, a couple of houses between them and the transmitter, where the quality of the reception dropped away but with the radio presenter still audible.

"The instructions reckon up to six hundred metres with line of sight and about 200 metres with stuff between, that seems to be what we have," said Luny.

"The street where I was thinking of parking is only about two hundred metres away from the house," said Dek. "There's a low hill in between but no houses, but it's not exactly line of sight. I can show you on the way home. Do you want to have some breakfast and head off."

"Yeah, let's get back." Luny's voice sounded a little tight from the excitement.

Luny crawled back under the house and eased the transmitter away from the flooring. He sat for a moment looking at the sticky pad thinking that it had held quite well but not convinced he would trust it enough to use again without some other assistance.

They packed up, locked the house and headed to the main street to a cafe where they had eaten breakfast on a previous visit and where, according to Dek, the coffee was of an acceptable quality.

Luny made no comment about Dek's meniscus.

Dek turned the car off the highway when they hit the outskirts of the city. It was only a short drive to the suburb and street where the clubhouse was situated.

"I feel a bit nauseous," said Dek, his breath coming out short and his voice tight, as they turned into the clubhouse street. "I'll just do one pass, it's the place on the bend up ahead, number twenty-one."

It was an innocuous three or four bedroom home built from light-coloured bricks and topped with a tile roof, like thousands of others in the city. But where you might normally find a bed of native flora, a strip of green lawn and a few garden gnomes out the front, this house had a dozen Harley Davidson motorcycles parked haphazardly on a patch of brown dirt.

"I've driven past a couple of times already," said Dek. "Not much activity during daylight on week days, sometimes there's one or two bikes there, but usually none. There's always a group there at night. I reckon we can do it from over the back fence."

Dek drove out of the u-shaped street, turning right onto the same road they had followed to find the clubhouse. He drove past the entrance they had used, turning into a cul-de-sac that ran parallel with the clubhouse street. The cul-de-sac ended in a children's playground.

"This is a good spot to listen from, if the device works," said Luny, "no houses in the street."

Parking in front of the playground, "Come and have a look," said Dek.

Reaching under his seat he pulled out a black case, and removed a pair of binoculars.

"Zildi?"

Dek loved Zildi, ignoring Luny's pointed comments about the irony of a man, obsessed with brand names, choosing to buy his groceries at an outlet specialising in home-brand products.

As far as Dek was concerned, shopping at Zildi, for him was striking a blow against the evil cartel of Australia's leading grocery outlets, who he accused vehemently of screwing customers with over-priced goods and underwhelming quality. Deep down he also thought it made him more interesting, like choosing to watch SBS television, Australia's multicultural network, in preference to the commercial offerings, a little bit bohemian if you like.

He loved his Zildi time. A first, quick sweep with the trolley to get his weekly supplies, and a slower, more leisurely cruise past the week's little surprises. Dek was constantly amazed at Zildi's capacity to offer, at sale price, goods that he wasn't even aware that he needed. Fair enough, he had not had a lot of opportunities to use the motorcycle helmet or the long-handled tree loppers but they were there if, and when required.

"Of course Zildi, Quality German engineering, at a sensible price."

Leaving the car Dek led Luny across the tanbark-covered playground and up a small rise to a stand of juvenile eucalypts growing on top of the knoll. They stopped in the trees.

"That's the place there, the one with the grills on the windows," said Dek—the tightness still evident in his voice—pointing to a house whose back fence was about fifty metres away across an open space covered in knee-length dry grass.

"This is the first good look I've had," he said, scanning the rear of the house. "They've got security system flashers and signs but I reckon it's those fake ones you can buy. Even if they are real, it won't matter because we won't be going near the entry doors or windows. They've got a standard-looking door to access beneath the floor. The problem is it has a padlock on it."

"Give me a look," said Luny, reaching for the binoculars. "We can buy a similar one and cut the old one," he said scanning the property. "Hopefully no-one will try to unlock it any time after we do it." Handing the binoculars back," Come on let's get out of here before someone notices us."

They sat in the car in a deafening silence, neither man moving.

Luny was the first to speak.

"Phew, that got the blood pumping a bit."

Dek let out a snort and burst out laughing.

"My heart rate is about two hundred." He paused and turned towards Luny, the doubt showing in his eyes. "Do you think we can do this?"

"Fuck it, what's the worst that can happen. Let's go

straight to a hardware shop and get a lock and some bolt cutters before we change our minds."

They pulled into a throbbing Saturday afternoon Tool Mart car park, the sound of overloaded shopping trolleys being dragged across bitumen, and the cry of happy and unhappy children and remonstrating parents, filling the air.

The smell of frying onions and sausages from the fund-raiser barbecue near the entrance did not help Dek's nausea.

"This is about the right size," said Luny, holding out a gold-coloured lock to Dek.

"Yep, looks the right size to me."

"Let's get a couple," said Luny, "I want to have a practice on one and see how hard it is to cut and how much noise it will make."

Dek was very glad that Luny was with him. He would never have thought of doing what Luny had suggested.

They moved to the tools area of the store and began looking through an assortment of bolt cutters.

"I haven't got a bloody clue what we should get," said Luny, looking around for someone to help him.

"I'll get someone," said Dek, thinking he could be of some use.

Spotting an older man in a Tool Mart apron

helping a customer further down the aisle, Dek loitered on the periphery of the conversation making eye contact with the man. Quickly raising his index finger to secure his place in line for the man's services before the couple coming from the other direction were able to beat him to the punch.

The man turned to Dek when he had finished with the previous customer.

"How can I help you?"

"I'd like your advice on bolt-cutters please," said Dek leading the man towards the spot where Luny was continuing to peruse an assortment of bolt cutters.

"Ah, hi," said Luny, "we want to cut a lock like this, what do we need?"

"You're not criminals are you?" said the man, looking straight Luny.

Luny was shocked and didn't know what to say. The old man smiled.

"Just kidding. You won't need anything like those that you're holding, a much smaller pair will do it."

The man pulled a couple of sets from the shelf.

"These are dearer and if you are wanting to use them regularly I'd recommend them," he said handing a pair of cutters to Luny, "but if it's a one-off job and occasional use then these will do just fine," the man said proffering a second pair.

"Just make sure when you use them that you push the shackle into the jaws of the cutters as far as they will go. Anything else?"

"No, that's great, thanks for your help," said Luny.

Back at Luny's, Luny looked closely at the cutters.

"I guess I'd better do the testing on this lock given I'm the bunny risking my life."

Dek felt awkward but couldn't think of anything useful to say.

Luny took a lock and placed the shackle between the jaws of the bolt cutters making sure he pushed the shackle in until it would go no further. Generating pressure on the handles, it was only a couple of seconds before the shackle gave way and the lock fell to the floor.

"Well, that was easy," he said.

"And not very noisy at all," Dek chipped in.

"Ok, the big question, when should we do it?"

"I reckon Tuesday night at around 3am," said Dek.

"Yeah, agreed. Most people are out to it at that time. I imagine it's even a quiet night for bikies."

"I know you'll laugh at me, but we should wear black and maybe balaclavas as well."

"What's this 'we' business?" enquired Luny.

"I'll be at the back fence with you."

"Well thanks heaps for the support."

"You should wear my overalls and I've got a balaclava for you," Dek said, wanting to feel that he was sharing the load. "The overalls have lots of pockets and hopefully won't snag on anything. What else do we need?"

"Nothing I can think of."

"Let's have a coffee on Monday and see if we've missed anything crucial," said Dek.

Dek departed, leaving Luny with the electronic equipment saying he would check it over and make sure it was fully charged and functioning.

5

Monday's coffee date rolled around and neither had thought of anything to add, apart from Luny suggesting he would take a can of lubricant to spray the hinges before he opened the door.

"That is assuming I haven't been perforated by twelve-gauge shots by that stage," he added, less in jest than he would have liked.

"Maybe we shouldn't do it," said Dek, suddenly worried for his friend.

"Don't fucking say that. We've gone this far, I'll always wonder about it if we don't at least get the device in. Nah, we're doing it, but let's go tonight, I can't bear another sleepless night."

"No, if we're going to do it, we need to stick to

our plan. We both thought that Tuesday was the best night, so let's trust our instincts," Dek said.

"Ok, Tuesday it is. But I'll leave it to you to inform the tax-paying citizens of this nation why they're not getting much constructive work out of me today and tomorrow."

"And that's different from the usual state of affairs, how?" said Dek, relishing an opportunity he rarely received.

Walking away, with a finger in the air, all Luny said was, "Fuck off."

Monday was okay for Luny, but for most of Tuesday, he was shitting bricks. The longer the day wore on, the larger grew the bricks. As he had predicted, he found it almost impossible to concentrate on his work. He was finding the waiting excruciating. His pulse raced and his guts quivered, threatening to explode with the rumble of fear he carried.

The plan was to go to bed on Tuesday night and sleep until two in the morning. Luny would pick up Dek—better they take a different vehicle, given Dek's Honda had been past the house a few times already.

Luny left work at three in the afternoon after lying to his boss that he had to take his mother to the doctor. He figured that a few hours of video gaming at home was far more beneficial to him than the pretext of working. Sliding into bed at ten-thirty, he didn't feel he'd slept for more than a few minutes by the time his alarm went off. Shrugging off the wave of tiredness, he dressed in Dek's overalls and tucked the black balaclava, that Dek had given him, into one of the pockets.

Dek looked bright. Luny suspected Dek would have slept well, knowing he wasn't the one who had to crawl under the house and risk having his arse blown away by an enraged bikie.

Neither said much during the twenty minute drive. The radio was on but turned down low barely audible above the noise of the tyres on the road. There was an occasional rustling as Dek moved his feet in the detritus that surrounded them. They were almost at the destination when Dek said, "So what do I do if something goes wrong, like if a bikie grabs you?"

"If for some reason a bikie grabs me, call the cops and get them here as quickly as you can. I don't see much point in doing anything else. I'd rather be trying to convince the cops that I was getting my soccer ball out of their yard than trying to convince a couple of angry bikies."

"Actually, I've thought about it, I reckon you

should just say we did it for a dare, trying to sneak in. Hopefully they won't find the device in your pocket."

"Yeah, that's not bad," acknowledged Luny. "Let's hope we don't have to use it. We'll do a drive-by on the house to see if anyone's there or if they're up and about before anything else.

All seemed quiet as they passed along the street, no bikes out front of the clubhouse or lights on in the house. They drove back to the playground in the cul-de-sac.

Even without his 'working' overalls to wear, Dek, had still managed to clad himself in a dark outfit. Sporting a pair of black, skinny jeans, black polo neck skivvy, topped with a black Billabong hoodie for once, he'd dressed so as not to be noticed. His only non-black dispensation was his brown-leather hiking boots, which he figured would not stand out in long grass.

Pushing the bolt cutters into the leg pocket of his overalls, Luny patted his pockets checking that he had the other bits and pieces.

Secreted in the trees at the top of the rise, they paused to see if there was any movement at any of the houses backing on to the hill. Satisfied that all was quiet, they moved through the grass to the back fence of the clubhouse.

Squatting down in the long grass they waited, having agreed to watch the house for five minutes to see or hear if there was any movement from inside. Luny lasted less than two minutes.

"I'm going to do it," he said in a hoarse whisper, pulling his balaclava from his pocket and tugging it over his face. Just as he started to move, the back door of the house opened and out stepped a bikie. Luny ducked down with adrenalin coursing through his veins. His heart thudded and for a brief moment, with the speed of his pulse he wondered if he'd blow an artery.

Frozen with fear they bent low into the grass and kept their faces down as footsteps approached the fence a couple of metres from where they hid.

The bikie stopped, undid his zip and the acrid smell of urine filled the air as he pissed all over the fence, some splashing through into the grass not far from Luny and Dek. The zip went up again and the footsteps retreated to the house. The distinct tread of boots on stairs and the door closing with a resounding thud told them the bikie was gone.

"Fuuuuuuuck," whispered Luny. "Fuuuuuck."

"Holy shiiiiit," was Dek's whispered response.

Both men collapsed onto their arses, backs against the fence.

"We'd better get out of here," whispered Dek.

"No fucking way," spat Luny. "I won't be able to do this again, it's now or never."

"You're fucking crazy," said Dek, using language he normally found coarse. "What if he hears you, it'll be death by a sawn-down gun-thingy like you said. I won't be able to do anything. I'll be too busy soiling myself over here behind the fence."

"If he got up to pee it means he must have been pissed when he went to bed," said Luny, thinking it out, his reasoning based primarily on his own behaviours. "He'll fall asleep again quickly. I've got to do it now. I won't have the cojones to do it again. I'm doing it. And it's sawn-off, not sawn-down."

"Alright, alright," whispered Dek. His throat so tight his words came out hoarse. Pulling Luny back to the ground, "Just give it ten minutes, give him time to go back to sleep, and then go."

"Ok, maybe my heart rate will be made up of individual beats by then. Fuuuuuck."

The ten minutes passed like hours, and it was all Luny could do to wait. Finally, he stood up and stared at the fence. One thing they hadn't thought about was how Luny was going to get over it. Luny stared at the palings which were higher than the top of his head.

"I hadn't thought about this."

"I'll have to help you," whispered Dek, linking his fingers together forming a cup.

Luny stepped in with his left foot. Dek let out a small groan as Luny raised his right leg, putting his full weight into Dek's hands. Luny grabbed the top of the palings with both hands, swinging his right leg up at the same time. Dek tried to stand to reduce the distance for Luny to reach his right leg to the top of the fence. It didn't work as well as Dek hoped.

While Luny's foot failed to reach its goal he did manage to snag the cuff of his overalls on top of a paling. He was caught, he couldn't go down or up and Dek was slowly losing the strength to bear Luny's weight. Luny could feel a stretch growing in his groin as his legs moved further part. Dek began to stagger under the load.

"I've got to put you down," Dek whispered.

"I can't do anything, my fucking foot's caught."

"I can't hold you. You're too heavy."

Dek's hands were getting lower and lower. Luny thought he about was a second away from tearing muscle and sinew as the pressure on his groin increased.

Dek gave no thought to Luny's groin, thinking only that Luny was about to crush his fingers against the ground if he didn't let go. Thankfully for both men, the cuff of the overalls could no longer take the load and released its grip on the top of the paling, depositing Luny on his back into the grass with a thud.

"Fuck," said Luny quietly through clenched teeth, more in frustration than pain. "Get on all fours," he commanded rolling onto his feet.

Dek didn't argue, settling himself in the long grass. Luny stepped up onto his arched back. Dek groaned but held fast. Luny reached for the top of the palings and lunged off Dek's back managing this time to get his right foot on top, hauling himself up, teetering precariously.

Realising there was nothing for it, he pushed forward, pitching over, plunging down towards the ground on the other side. If climbing the fence had been arduous and time-consuming, his plummit back to *terra firma* was something else entirely. He was at Mach five by the time he contacted the ground. Thankfully the yard sloped down towards the house. He struck the ground and unintentionally rolled several times before coming to a stop, face down.

As winded as he felt, fear drove Luny to his feet. Like a beach sprinter at a surf carnival, he was up and at the back wall of the house in record time, expecting at any moment for the door to be flung open and for him to be staring into the murderous twin orbs of a sawn-off shotgun.

Crouched and paused, Luny's pulse roared in his ears. He took a breath, and then held the next, listening for any sounds from inside the house. Hearing nothing, he exhaled, waiting a minute or so to get his breathing under control, before turning and placing the padlock shackle in the jaws of his bolt cutters.

"God bless the old man at Tool Mart," he whispered aloud, as the shackle gave way easily and quietly.

He put the broken lock in one of the many pockets of his overalls, and pulled out a small can of lubricant from another. He coated the gate hinges and the lock hasp in a long, solid squirt, waiting a further minute or so for the liquid to do its work.

He pulled the hasp away from the plate of the locking mechanism, meaning that the door could now swing open. The hinges didn't utter a squeak. The only sound the door made was that of the dried brown grass being pushed out of the way as Luny pulled the gate over the top of it.

Replacing the lube in his pocket Luny pulled out a head-torch from another pocket. Sucking in a deep breath, he crawled inside the darkness and pulled the door shut behind him before switching on the light.

He swung the beam around and was relieved to see that that the underside of the house was clear of rubbish that might thwart his passage. All he could see were the standard brick pillars and beams that formed the underside of most houses. The one thing he hadn't counted on was under floor insulation. He briefly pondered the notion of bikies being concerned with mundane issues such as energy efficiency in the home. However, he realised that this might actually be a positive in helping him to conceal the device.

He had discussed with Dek the most likely spot to pick up conversation. From the street it appeared that the lounge room, like many Canberra homes of this style, was at the front of the house facing the street. This seemed to the both of them the most likely place for conversations to occur. Unfortunately for Luny it was at the diagonally opposite end of the house from where he'd entered.

The floor was close enough to the ground that Luny wasn't able to scrabble along on hands and knees and was forced to leopard-crawl the whole way. He was surprised, and very happy, that there weren't any spider webs in his path. However, it was the ones that lived on the ground that troubled him more, like funnel webs. He was pretty sure that only Sydney funnel webs were deadly but he wasn't keen to prove his theory, and was thankful to Dek, for the protection of his overalls.

Adrenalin helped him to make light work of the crawling, as stopped at what he thought would be the centre of the front room. He rolled onto his back and pulled the device from a pocket. Switching it to the 'on' position, he felt the new replacement sticky pad was good. As an added precaution against the transmitter coming unstuck he also had a couple of thick rubber bands and thumbtacks. Finding a gap between two insulation batts, he pushed them apart to reveal the floorboards above. With a solid grip, he pushed the device against the flooring and released it. The tape held it in place. He then pinned a rubber band to the floor and stretched it over the device pinning it again on the other side. He repeated the process with the second rubber band.

Satisfied that the device was secure, he pushed the batts back into place, turned, and slithered carefully towards the entrance, switching off his headlamp before opening the door. Once outside he shut the small door, pulled the new lock from his pocket and secured it in place and then made sure there were no tell-tale signs of incursion in the grass around the door.

He crouched and ran to the back fence. This time he had two cross rails with which to gain purchase and managed to scramble over the fence unassisted, dropping into the grass beside Dek.

"Fuuuuuuck," he whispered, "lets get out of here."

The two men moved briskly back through the long grass to the playground and to Luny's car.

"Holy fuck, I never want to do that again. It's cold and the sweat is running down my arse crack."

"Nice work, let's turn it on and make sure it registers before we get too far away," said Dek.

Safe in the car Dek pushed and held the 'on' button on the receiver for the requisite five seconds. They both breathed a sigh of relief when the red light glowed warmly, alerting them that the under-house transmitter was working.

Dek switched the receiving unit off again and packed it away.

"Let's get the fuck away from here," said Luny, starting the engine.

They were almost out of the cul-de-sac when Dek asked, "Where are the bolt cutters?"

Luny slammed on his brakes and looked across

at Dek, "I left them in the fucking grass beside the door."

"Turn around, I'll get them," said Dek. Luny drove back to the playground.

Dek said firmly, "Wait here."

He was back in less than two minutes, panting and throwing the bolt cutters onto the back seat. "Let's go."

Luny stared at his friend with something approaching awe. "Thanks for that."

After a brief pause Dek said, "Next time we may need to rethink our fence scaling techniques."

Both men snorted with laughter, enjoying the release of tension.

"Imagine what would have happened if you hadn't stopped me going earlier."

Dek shivered.

"Let's not think about that."

It was four-thirty when Luny parked outside Dek's home. "Coffee tomorrow," were his departing words.

Luny was home soon after. He ripped off the overalls and collapsed into bed, the adrenalin long-since dissipated, exhaustion replacing it.

"Now we just have to go down there and sit until we learn something useful," said Dek.

They were back at the work coffee-haunt the next day. The dark rings around their eyes showed that both men were feeling the effects of what had occurred only a few hours previously.

"I'm stuffed from last night, let's start taking it in turns from tomorrow night. How should we do it?" asked Luny.

"I reckon we drive past the house at around seven and see if anyone's parked there, if they are, then drive over and tune in from near the playground," said Dek.

"If we start driving past the house regularly we might get noticed, you've already been past in your car a few times."

"Fair point. What about parking at the playground, are locals likely to get suspicious?"

"Shame we can't rent a kid. It might be better if we were both there together, then we'd just look like a couple of gays having a snog," said Luny. "The nearest houses are a few hundred metres away, let's just do a few nights each at the playground and see what happens, and then we can look for some other spots around the house where we can pick up the signal."

"Good plan," said Dek, noticing, not for the first time, that the conversations between him and Luny of late were very civil and respectful—a little unnerving he thought.

"Alright, I'll go first if you like, starting tomorrow night," said Luny, enthusiasm obvious in his tone, "I want to see if the gear will work."

Luny had given a bit of thought to the discussion he and Dek had about keeping a low profile in the area around the clubhouse. Luny thought his car with all its dents and missing parts might be something that people would remember if they saw it more than once. He decided to ask his brother if he could borrow a car, giving the reason that his Falcon was getting repaired.

He could have asked his mum, which wouldn't have been a problem, but Luny wasn't keen on his mother getting involved in any sort of trouble.

However, he had no such compunction where his brother was concerned. He didn't spend a lot of time with his brother, largely because he thought him a bit of a tosser, who took great delight in finding fault with Luny at every, and any opportunity.

His brother was a partner in a busy law practice in Canberra and loved nothing better than gloating to Luny about the trappings of his successful career. This included the trophy wife, a massive house with pool and tennis court in the right suburb, and kids with braces in private school. And there were the regular overseas holidays.

Luny actually liked his brother's wife a lot and wondered how she put up with the knob she had married. He figured money took away some of the pain. Luny also enjoyed hanging with his nephews who both loved to talk electronics and gaming with their quirky uncle. He would have liked to spend more time with them but it unfortunately involved seeing his brother.

And of course, as Luny predicted, the price of borrowing his brother's car, was a ten-minute lecture on why he shouldn't be driving around in an old wreck. Luny took it on the chin, as he had so many times before, and grinned inwardly at the ruckus it would create in his brother's world if he were somehow connected to a bikie-related crime. It would be almost worth getting caught, thought Luny, almost.

The car was a white hatchback that the *au pair* used to run to the shops and deliver kids to school. But as the whole family was heading to Europe for three weeks, including the *au pair*, his brother was happy for him to borrow it until their return, with the parting proviso that he not treat it as he did his own car. Luny was relieved he had not offered one of the matching Audis that he and his wife drove.

As Luny headed off for the first listening session he felt relaxed and excited. He and Dek had reasoned that it was very unlikely that the bikies could find them even if they discovered the device so Luny was a little more comfortable as he parked near the playground a second time. The fact that no one was using the park made him feel even better. He was concerned about being noticed and someone calling the police suspecting he was a pedophile.

Parking the car facing out of the cul-de-sac, allowed Luny to be ready for a quick departure if necessary. He would stay as long as he could hear conversation, capturing it all on a digital audio recorder he had bought for the purpose. Even though his pulse had quickened a little at the prospect of tuning in for the first time, Luny first got himself settled before switching on the receiver. He placed his thermos, sandwiches and Pringles in accessible positions and then finally switched the receiver to the 'on' position. He could hear conversation. The machine really was very good.

6

At the same time that Luny was breathing a big sigh of relief that the receiver was working, in the garage of a house two hundred metres in the other direction from the club, Constable Octavia Rider, an officer of the Canberra Federal Police force, was also making herself comfortable for an evening of eavesdropping.

The night before Luny's early morning incursion under the clubhouse, the same activity was undertaken by the Canberra Police, placing a listening device less than a metre from where Luny had hidden his device. Padlock sales in Canberra were going through the roof.

The police had set up camp in a garage belonging to the sister of one of their senior officers and had not needed to station someone in a vehicle near the playground as had been one of the options discussed.

The Narcotics Branch had ramped up both their numbers and their efforts in response to the growing problem of drugs—chiefly methamphetamines or ice as it was universally known—in and around the national capital. They were aware that local bikie groups, the Satan's Mongrels chief among them, were attempting to build their presence in the local drugs market.

Thanks to a bit of judicious strong-arming of a small-fry dealer the police were aware that the Satan's Mongrels were planning a large 'buy' of pseudoephedrine, a key ingredient in the manufacture of ice. The information was reliable enough to enable the police to secure the necessary permissions to place a listening device beneath the Mongrels' clubhouse.

Constable Rider had volunteered for the listening shift for the remainder of the week and over the weekend and would stay in place each night until she was sure there was no one left in the clubhouse to overhear. She had the phone number of some senior detectives if there was anything urgent to report. Rider liked this.

Rider was a young and very ambitious police

officer. She pushed for every job which might get her noticed by those above, particularly those moving in plain-clothed circles. These efforts did not endear her to her peers, who saw her as a brown-noser and a lone wolf. Rider knew this and could not have cared less.

Rider had always been a loner. She was an only child, the product of older parents who had long given up on the idea of having children. When little Octavia had happened along she was largely seen as an impediment to well-established and independent lifestyles.

Her mother, a keen student of Roman history, had named her Octavia after the sister of the first Roman Emperor, Augustus, and fourth wife of Mark Antony.

By the time she was four she understood that she shared a name with one of the most prominent women in Roman history, a woman who was respected and admired by contemporaries for her loyalty, nobility and humanity, and for maintaining traditional Roman feminine virtues.

By the time she was six, following a gradual increase in teasing by her classmates, the name had lost much of its lustre and she wished she could change it. It didn't help her friendship prospects that her parents treated her like an adult from a young age, making it very difficult for little Octavia to mix with other children. She learned from an early age to enjoy her own company.

Octavia was always one of the top students in her year through both primary and high school. She could have studied almost anything at any of Australia's universities. But to her parents' horror, Octavia chose to join the police force. It wasn't a rash decision, Rider had made up her mind years before, following a presentation by two police officers at her school.

She had loved the power that the uniform exuded from the moment the police officers walked through the door. The self-confidence it gave to the officers sold the idea further to Octavia. Following some research, she realised that there was even greater power to be enjoyed by those in the plain-clothed police.

When she had submitted her application she had never felt such excitement. While there was little doubt that the service would refuse someone of her capabilities she still waited anxiously for the response.

When the invitation arrived she had danced around her bedroom in delight. Her training had gone much the same way as her primary and high school education. The trainers were initially concerned about her reluctance to engage with other trainees but were impressed by her academic achievements and her motivation.

Her fellow trainees quickly learned to avoid her. She graduated top of her ear, with few friends, loads of enemies and with a focused direction to succeed.

It took very little time for Octavia to establish herself as an extremely bright and intuitive young police officer in the eyes of her superiors. The fact that she was viewed with suspicion, and mistrust by her peers, didn't bother her.

She could not have cared less. She had only had one focus, and that was to move up the promotion ladder as quickly as possible.

Rider wasn't quite as organised as Luny and was munching Doritos and sipping a ginger beer when the first voices could be heard over her receiver. She made sure the recording device was working and stopped munching, leaning back into the camping chair to listen.

The police had a dossier on all the main members of the club, with the club's leader in Canberra, Tony Ellery—or Fist as he was known in the Mongrels—their main person-of-interest.

Having spent most of his life in Sydney it was the NSW Police which had provided the majority of the information they held on Ellery. Apart from more than a few assault-related and dope charges in his youth Ellery had managed to keep himself out of the courts and police custody for many years.

The ACT Police knew he played a major role in managing several brothels in Canberra. But it wasn't these legal businesses which the Police were interested in, it was the growing ice trade in the national capital and suspicions of Mongrels' role in that.

Ellery's road name, Fist, wasn't a coincidence. He was known as a strong-arm enforcer who was not afraid to break heads. It had quickly became obvious to the police that Ellery was a man both respected and feared by those who knew him.

More than a few people had commented over the years that Fist resembled a taller and slightly more youthful version of Willie Nelson. Fist was comfortable with the comparison, being a big fan of the man's music.

Fist wore his salt-and-pepper hair pulled back and plaited into a ponytail tied off with a leather thong. While the crow's feet around his eyes and the weathered and blueish hue of his skin made him look older than his years it also gave him an air of authority and competence.

Fist was old school. One of a dying breed in the bikie clubs, and he knew it. It worried him now that the focus was so much on money and profit. He mourned the passing of the old days of group rides and wild drunken weekends and lots of sex. It had been a much more carefree existence. Now it was all business.

Half the fuckers don't even ride hogs any more, he'd occasionally say to his wife after a few too many Jack-and-cokes. It was the old values that were being eroded he would say. It used to be club first and nothing else. From the outside, people might have viewed them as wild and unruly, and they were, but within a strict code and hierarchy. Anyone stepping out of line was likely to face the brunt of Fist's wrath. And Fist hadn't earned his road name by chance.

But for Fist those times seemed to be slipping away. More and more he saw, especially in Sydney and Melbourne, new people brought in without having served their time before becoming fully-fledged members. They didn't prove their allegiance and that is what truly upset, and concerned Fist the most.

To die for his colours, was how deep Fist's loyalty ran. Backed by many scars of battle from fist, boot, knife and even bullet, he was a loyal club man to the core. These young fuckers today, he would tell his wife, just wanted it handed to them. He didn't trust them.

He was happy when it was suggested he move to Canberra a few years before. While he missed the big city he was happy to get out of the politics of Sydney club membership and build a small chapter in the national capital. For a while it was a return to the good old days, nothing more than a bit of dope, hookers, debt-collection and stand-over activity, but that had changed.

The Canberra chapter of the Mongrels wasn't large, with only a dozen members. But this was how the Sydney management wanted it. Just enough muscle, to get the work done without attracting too much attention. Numbers were topped up as necessary from other chapters, usually from Sydney, which was less than three hours away by Harley.

Sydney was very happy with how things were going in Canberra. The demand for ice in the nation's capital had surprised everyone. But rather than continue to move product in from Sydney and Melbourne—particularly when law enforcement agencies were watching so closely—a Canberra-based manufacturing unit was being trialled, and run completely independently from the Sydney operation.

A recently graduated chemical engineer with a habit, had been contracted to cook the product at a farm on the outskirts of the city. Fist kept a close eye on him. The idea of trusting a coke head with so much responsibility did not sit well with Fist, particularly as his own future was at risk if the boy fucked up.

Despite his concerns, Fist had to admit that the set-up was working well, a fact that was not overlooked by the powers in Sydney. Like all good illegal operations Fist kept the process as simple as possible, involving a minimal number of people. The biggest challenge was getting a regular supply of pseudoephedrine, the key ingredient in making ice. The days had long past when needs could be met by employing runners to buy up products containing pseudoephedrine, like Sudafed, from chemist shops. On top of the issue of quantity, chemists now asked questions, sought identification and took names. So Sydney had begun sourcing the product offshore with supplies made available to Canberra when required, rarely affecting production.

Such was the success of the Canberra operation, Sydney thought the time had come to increase the payloads of pseudoephedrine so that delivery frequency could be reduced, minimising the risk of detection from prying eyes.

Fist had been called to Sydney to receive his instructions and the cash needed for the buy. This kind of conversation did not happen over the telephone.

Kicking back in the car listening had been a buzz for Luny. The element of doing something illegal had given him a rush, and the conversations he'd heard had been akin to an audio porn book. While he hadn't learned much of value—other than the fact that bikies enjoyed beer, women, fighting and Harleys—he had already begun to get a sense of some of the different personalities. He started to feel more like an anthropologist than someone looking for clues as to the whereabouts of large amounts of cash.

It was pretty obvious to Luny from the outset that the guy called Fist was in charge. While the other bikies joked around with him, as they did with each other, Luny could feel the restraint and respect in their voices when they addressed him.

And they all had nicknames. To Luny it sounded like a child's first reader, with names like Dog, Rope and Spanner. And some others you might not find in a Spot book, like Turd and Fist.

Luny stayed until just after eleven when the bikies had all gone their separate ways. Heading back along the cul-de-sac, he stopped, giving way to a car before turning on to the next street. He may have been a little perturbed had he known the other car was being driven by Octavia Rider.

Rider, similarly had enjoyed her first night of listening, more so because of the pat on the head she received from the boss when she called him at eleven. She had been in two minds about calling so late with such a small detail but her instincts had not failed her. She had explained that Ellery was heading to Sydney the next day but hadn't said why. The boss had thanked her and said she had shown good judgement in calling, reinforcing that she should call with any detail she thought might be relevant. She was a very happy constable on the drive home.

Home was a new one-bedroom, apartment on the third-floor right in the centre of Canberra. She owned the apartment thanks to the generosity of her parents.

Rider felt that the apartment was her parents' way of washing their hands of her, still unable to accept her career choice. She saw her unit as a final debt paid. She was comfortable with that.

Her focus was solely on her work. Keen to progress, she had little time for the social niceties, rarely accepting invitations to parties or other social occasions if she was asked.

Her piercing green eyes, olive skin and auburn hair complemented a physique that Rider worked hard in the gym to maintain. Her butt was tight and her breasts were pert and that is how she intended they remain for many years to come. She knew that her looks were part of her path to success.

She had rebuffed the advances of more than a few of the junior males from her training group who had quickly branded her a lesbian. She heard the snickers but cared little. She wasn't a lesbian and quite liked sex but there was no way she was going to waste her time with an officer at her own level, she saw little value in this.

She had one tenuous friendship with a similarly aged woman who worked in forensics. They had met in the police gym. They occasionally went for dinner or a movie but the limited frequency had reduced even further when the woman had started a relationship with another officer.

Rider was comfortable with this. She was happy

with her own company and rarely felt the pangs of loneliness. She knew that respect and interaction would come when she moved into the more senior levels, and this would only be a matter of time as far as she was concerned.

7

Luny and Dek had a coffee the next day to discuss what had transpired.

"Nothing of use but it was really interesting," said Luny with much enthusiasm. "The device worked a treat, we've obviously got it in the right place. All they did was drink beer, talk about sex and Harleys. They left around eleven and so did I."

"I love it," said Dek. "They sit there drinking all night and then ride those stupid motorcycles home. Where's the booze bus to stop these tossers."

Luny ignored the outburst.

"The guy in charge seems to be a bloke called Fist. The only thing I learned was that he's off to Sydney today but didn't say why. You'll go tonight?" Luny asked.

"Yep, my turn," said Dek. "I'll meet you for brunch at the usual time tomorrow."

"They talked about some sort of party tonight," said Luny. "If it's rowdy it might be hard to hear anything."

Rowdy was an understatement thought Dek as he sat in his car beside the playground that night. He wondered what the neighbours must be going through, not that they would knock on the door to complain or call the police. Dek could actually hear the noise from the house coming up and over the hill without the need of the receiver.

He was considering his options when a set of headlights lit up his face, a car was driving towards him. Dek's heart went into overdrive in an instant. He swore out loud, fumbling the listening gear down onto the floor on the passenger side, knocking over his newly opened bottle of coke, which had been sitting on the arm rest between the seats.

He glanced up to see the car moving very slowly towards him. Dek was frantic, turning to look into the back seat, looking for something to cover the device. There was nothing there. He pulled his jumper over his head and through it down, on top of the gear. His head shot back up as he sat there staring ahead with his hands at nine and three on the steering wheel, clenching tightly, like he was doing his driving test with an instructor in the car. He could not have looked more guilty.

The car finally reached him, driving past to do a u-turn in the end of the cul-de-sac behind him. Dek didn't dare turn his head, staring sideways as the car drove past. All he saw was a young couple staring at him.

The car didn't stop, driving back past Dek and along the street and out of sight.

Dek let out a massive breath, restarting his breathing. His heart was pounding in his ears.

"Holy shit," he said out loud.

He turned to see the last dregs of his coke gurgling onto the carpet of the floor in the back seat.

He retrieved the listening device. All he could hear was loud music and loud voices, but nothing discernible. He packed up and drove off, leaving behind the pounding lyrics of Bond Scott and the boys. For a brief moment he was tempted to call the police and complain about the noise but thought better of it.

On the drive home he decided not to tell Luny of his escapades but vowed silently that he would be better organised for such an eventuality in the future.

Given his short stint, Dek told Luny that he would do the Saturday night shift as well. This suited Luny, as it left him free to attend a party that Stella had only told him about that morning.

That night, as Dek listened, his heart-rate went into orbit again, but for a very different reason.

Rider's reaction wasn't much different, only that she dropped the bag of Doritos she had nibbled at two nights before, the orange triangles spilling over her pants and onto the concrete floor of the garage. Rider grabbed her note pad and began to scribble furiously.

"I want you four to pick up the pseudo," said Fist.

Fist and four of the Mongrels were sitting in the front room of the clubhouse. The order and cleanliness inside the clubhouse would likely have surprised many people from outside the gang. The rooms were spartan but neat, and tidy with blinds on every window, and the walls clean and painted in neutral tones. Harley related artwork graced the walls that Fist had required to be framed and hung in a professional manner.

Fist also had very strict views on behaviour and order when it came to the clubhouse. Alcohol and pot were the only substances Fist permitted to be consumed inside the clubhouse. While he was happy for gang members and their guests to party hard he would not tolerate any sort of behaviour which might result in damage to the premises. To him this was showing disrespect to their colours.

On several occasions he had dealt out punishment for transgressors. Spanner, for example, had spent a recent weekend replacing plaster board in a wall he had punched a hole through when he was pissed. As a punishment Fist had made him repaint the whole lounge area.

Fist insisted that the place be cleaned top to bottom once a week, a paid job that fell to the wife of one of the gang members.

The front room was large and open and housed a range of sofas and recliners. A huge television was mounted on one wall with an expensive stereo system and speakers sitting against another. As Luny, Dek and the ACT Police had correctly guessed the bulk of club-related business was discussed in this room.

"The buy's set for next Thursday, at Eden wharf. There's been a bit of chatter around this deal. If anyone is watching I want to lead them away. I'll head down towards Nowra along the back roads through Nerriga with a few of the boys in a car."

Fist stood and looked out through the front window, speaking with his back to the four men.

"You guys go separately to Cooma on your bikes, meet up at ten at the road-house in the industrial area and head to the buy. Don't ride through Cooma, use the back way, the way we rode last summer for the piss-up at the coast, the dirt road from Bibbenluke to Cathcart and down Mt Darragh. You shouldn't see any cops on that road. Come back the same way."

Fist spun on his heal and locked eyes with one of the men.

"Turd, you're in charge and I want you to carry the cash. I don't have to tell you what'll happen if you fuck this up. It's the biggest pseudo buy we've done so the pressure's on from Sydney to get it right."

"You need to be at the cafe near the wharf at twelve. Get a table and have a coffee. You'll be approached. They'll take you to a quiet spot and you can do the swap.

Fist punched his left hand with his right several times, each punch in time with his points.

"Trust your instincts, if you get a sniff of a problem get the fuck out, look after the cash. You'll all need to carry. I'll get some pieces to you over the weekend."

"There should be eight bags, two kilos in each. But don't worry too much about checking weights, we'll do that here. They won't fuck us around, they wouldn't dare."

"That's a fair bit of gear, so make sure you all take saddle bags and split it up between you. Stay together on the way home and ride fuckin' sensibly. You get stopped with this and we won't be seeing you for a long time. It'll be a damn site longer if I get my hands on you."

Dek didn't know whether he should pee his pants with excitement or soil them in fear. He couldn't believe it had happened.

He wanted to call Luny straight away but calmed himself and remembered their agreement not to discuss anything specific over the phone. Dek didn't know what to do, should he wait and listen, or get back to Luny's place with the news? He decided that he had better hang around in case there were any other details.

Rider was just as excited. Her big opportunity was coming. She could feel it. Regaining her composure, she sucked in a series of deep breaths. She felt like she was warming down after a gym session. Feeling her racing heart slow, she dialled the head of the

Narc Branch to tell him the news. The boss was very happy.

Dek sat, wriggling with excitement but stuck it out for another hour. Nothing further of interest had been said. Music was played and beers were being drunk but that was about it. At ten o'clock his excitement got the better of him and he headed to Luny's house. Realising that if they were going to actually go through with this, they needed to plan quickly. It was Saturday and the deal was happening on the following Thursday in Eden.

Dek frowned when he found Luny's front door locked. He rapped on it with enthusiasm keen keen to tell Luny what he knew. When he got no response Dek thumped harder. "Damn, where are you Luny?" he said. Pulling his phone from his pocket, he remembered Luny saying something about a party.

He dialled Luny's number, thinking he would not reveal any details of the operation over a phone line, as per the agreement. There was very little chance of this when Stella answered Luny's mobile.

"Hi Dek, it's Stella," she said in a friendly voice.

"Hi Stella, can I please speak to Dek."

"It's your boyfriend," Dek heard Stella say as she passed the mobile to Luny.

"Hey," said Luny.

Even with the excitement of what he had learned at the bikie club, Dek couldn't hide his annoyance at having to speak to Stella and to hear her say what she had.

"Why's she answering your mobile?"

"I didn't want to carry it, so I put it in her handbag."

"It's on," Dek paused for effect, "we need to talk," the excitement had quickly returned after the brief Stella-moment diversion. "Tonight, we need to talk tonight."

"Can't it wait until morning, it's almost eleven o'clock, we won't be able to get anything done tonight. And we shouldn't be having this chat."

Luny's response was a bucket of cold water on Dek's enthusiasm.

"Didn't you hear me, it's happened, it's on."

"Ok, I get it, but there's nothing we can do tonight."

"Fine. Are you staying with her tonight?"

"Yep, and we're having brunch with some people in the morning as well, I doubt I can see you much before lunch time. I'll come over as soon as I can tomorrow. See you later." Luny broke the connection before Dek had a chance to respond.

Dek was seething. He pressed Luny's number again. But before it range, he swore, pressing the disconnect button as hard as he could.

Fine, he thought, stomping down the stairs, just fine.

8

"Ah, it's you," said Dek opening the door to Luny and glancing at his thin Skagen watch—another tribute to his love of things Scandinavian. "Better late than never I guess," he added turning away.

"Fuck off Dek," Luny rarely let Dek get away with his bitchy comments without a retort.

"It's on," said Dek as Luny plonked onto Dek's white leather couch.

Dek had slept late, in spite of the mixed emotions he had experienced the previous night. A Sunday morning spent thinking of options, ideas and potential outcomes, had rekindled his excitement.

"Yes, I believe you made that quite clear last night."

Dek ignored Luny's remark.

"It's on. I can't believe it. I'd only been listening for five minutes and it happened. They're doing a deal next Thursday. They're buying pseudoephedrine, the stuff they use to make ice. I Googled it, " said Dek thinking Luny would be impressed. "It's hard to get and really expensive to buy in large quantities."

Luny sat quietly without saying a word, a little ashen-faced at the prospect that an opportunity had so quickly presented itself. He'd never truly believed it would get to this point. He figured that placing the bug and listening in on the conversations of large, tattooed men would be enough of a thrill for both of them, providing fodder for whispered conversations, and knowing glances for years to come.

He had thought they would tire quickly of driving the twenty minutes each way to listen in, and eventually the battery would run down in the transmitter and it would just become a good story.

Dek finished explaining all that he had heard, and passed his recorder to Luny to hear it for himself.

"Did they mention how much cash they'd be carrying?" asked Luny.

"Wasn't mentioned."

"Then how do we know if it's worth it?"

"All I know is they said it was the biggest thing they had done and the leader was very worried that they protect the cash. It has to be a substantial amount."

"I don't want to risk my life for a pittance," argued Luny.

"Look, I have no idea but I have a feeling it's a good amount. We're never going to get a better opportunity."

"What constitutes a good amount? How much is enough to make it worthwhile risking our lives? Putting in the listening device was a bit of lark compared to this."

Dek didn't respond, he just sat staring towards the opposite wall.

Luny stared at Dek but then snapped from his reverie: "Get on Google Maps, what's the road they're talking about?".

"That's my old stomping ground," said Dek. "It's a back way to Eden, avoiding the larger towns.

"I'm guessing they must want to stay away from any police," said Luny.

"Yes, that's what Fist said, and he's also worried that people might know about the deal and might be watching him. He's going to head to a different part of the coast in case anyone's following, and leave the deal to four of the others."

"Well if someone is watching I hope they take

the bait and follow him," said Luny. "And what if they don't. We don't want to be dealing with two enemies. Who's watching, is it other bikies or cops or a fucking Chinese triad?"

Dek gulped.

"I hadn't really thought about that. Is this getting too complicated?" Dek asked.

"Look it wasn't like we were going to find the money in a bag on the side of the road, we were always going to have to earn it," said Luny. "Let's just see if we can put something together. We can make a decision then, weigh up a few risks."

"Alright, what do we know?" asked Dek rhetorically. "We know how many are going, and we know the route they're taking. A large section of it is on a quiet road through the bush, there's got to be an opportunity along there somewhere."

Tossing a few ideas around, both agreed that they would have to try and stop all four bikes together without raising suspicion, in a quiet spot where they could do their work quickly. They both came to the same conclusion that they would have to be armed.

Three hours later they had the rudiments of a plan. They agreed to meet after work the next day, Monday, to look at the plan again, and if agreed to start to execute the details.

9

The ACT police had also made a constructive start. They needed to move quickly. Plans were organised to contact their counterparts in the Federal Police and the NSW police, and get together to formulate a plan to intercept both the buyer and seller.

It was quickly established that the police response would take place in Eden, wherever the exchange took place. The plan would be simple. Monitor the Mongrels along the way, keeping well back, and having eyes on the ground in Eden to pick up and follow the buyer, and seller once they got together for the exchange.

Rider was not privy to these discussions and was worried that the planning might be going ahead without her. She didn't bother communicating with any of her superiors in uniform before heading upstairs and speaking to Senior Detective Ross Plumber, the detective she had dealt with during her monitoring activities.

"Boss?" Rider said, pushing into his office. "Boss, I'm keen to be involved in the drug op."

"Look Rider, I've said how much I appreciate your efforts on this but this is really a matter for us, the Feds and the NSW cops now, there's not really a role for uniform from this end."

"Boss, with respect, I feel like I have a stake in this and I can be of benefit, I know the bikies better than anyone. I really would like to follow it through."

"What does Nolan say?" Plumber asked referring to Rider's boss, Senior Sergeant Bob Nolan.

"I was hoping you might have a word with him."

"I've got to admire your balls, Rider, if you'll pardon the expression. I'll see what I can do."

"Thanks Boss."

"Stop calling me boss," Plumber said to Rider's departing back.

Plumber sighed and picked up the phone to call Bob Nolan, Rider's actual boss.

One person who didn't know where or how the buy was taking place, but who had an inkling that it was going down, was the President of the local chapter of the Ferals Motorcycle Club. The Ferals were the other major player in the bikie crime scene in Canberra. An ever-increasing tension over drug turf, saw the Ferals and the Mongrels coming to blows more and more frequently.

The President of the Ferals, Argo as he was known—a name he had adopted from the movie of the same name—had picked up information that suggested a big deal was in the offing for the Mongrels. He was almost certain his supplier was playing both sides of the street, selling pseudo to both clubs.

He knew the buy was happening soon—his supplier had gone cold on him, telling him nothing was available at the moment. He would keep an eye on Fist and some of the other senior Mongrels around town.

Luny and Dek met after work at their city coffee haunt. Dek was so preoccupied with the task ahead that he made no reference to the fact they were not able to secure their favourite table.

Dek laid A4 pages on the table.

"I wonder how many major crime syndicates use Excel spreadsheets complete with colour coding to plot their fiendish intent," said Luny when he had perused Dek's efforts.

"Hey, you're the one that says it's all in the planning."

"I hope you haven't saved the files anywhere that the cops or someone else can find them."

"Shit, I hadn't thought of that," said Dek, feeling more than a little stupid at such an obvious mistake.

"Shit Dek, how could you overlook that?"

"Don't worry, I'll get it off."

Seeing the pale colour of Dek's face, Luny backed off, "Don't panic, I was just joking, but it's probably a good idea to get rid of any evidence before we do this."

"Okay," said Dek, thankful for Luny's response but still feeling slightly nauseous from his rookie error.

"So we agree the plan is the best we can arrange with the time we have."

"Yep," said Luny.

The spread-sheet showed an action list itemising two white work utes (with roof flashers), orange overalls and hardhats, balaclavas, three 'road-closed' and one 'detour' sign, a pair of hand-held radios and two guns.

Dek had blanched visibly when Luny had explained he could get two twelve-gauge shotguns.

Luny's brother was a clay pigeon shooter, as Luny had been in his youth thanks to a father who had introduced both brothers to the sport at a young age. Luny no longer shot, and hadn't done so since he was seventeen. His brother saw it as a suitable pursuit for someone in his position and pursued the sport with his typical fanaticism, spending money on a collection of expensive weaponry which he kept, legally, in a gun safe at his house.

Fortunately, Luny knew that his brother had left a set of house keys at their mother's house.

"Dickhead's away with the family for ten days, so I can grab the guns tonight. I was thinking I would load some cartridges with rock-salt. If we have to make a point early on we can hit them without killing them. But we'll need to keep some regular cartridges handy in case it gets serious. We'll have double barrels so maybe we'll have one rock-salt and one regular shot in each."

"I really don't know what you just said, but I'm happy to discuss it at the coast," said Dek. "Did you sort your leave?"

"Yeah, I just said I had a bit of a family issue and asked for the rest of the week off, no problem."

"What did you tell Stella?" Dek almost choked over the name as he said it.

"I haven't told her yet, she hasn't called this week."

"So you're not allowed to call her?"

The question, unanswered, hung in the air between them.

"Look, you need to do something. We don't want her calling at some inopportune point," said Dek.

"Yeah, yeah, I'll sort it tonight, don't worry about it," was Luny's terse response.

Dek knew he had pushed a little hard and changed the subject.

"I got the third degree from the Shark. She didn't want to let me go and started asking for details. I had to lie and say my father was really sick. What a bitch."

"I've booked two Hilux utes, from different car hire places, one under your name and one under mine, as you suggested," Dek continued. "We can pick them up first thing tomorrow and then run around and get the rest of the stuff. I figure we can head off to Merimbula in the afternoon."

It had been agreed that the base of operations would be the Merimbula house.

Dek drove Luny to the first car hire office early the next morning to get the first ute. Luny had suggested renting from two separate firms, using two separate credit cards, just in case anyone started nosing around looking for someone who had hired two utes.

They dropped Dek's car at his house and picked up the second ute.

Like the vehicles, they agreed to buy their 'work wear' from separate shops. Luny had warned Dek not to make a fuss about bad fashion and poor fitting when he bought his gear. "You don't want this guy to remember you, get it?"

Each purchased orange overalls, and a white hard hat. Luny had bought hand-held UHF radios the day before—agonising for a long time over the relative merits of UHF versus VHF—from one of the large electronic outlets.

The final task before departing Canberra was to go back to Luny's place to retrieve the shotguns and the road-closed and detour signs.

They had had stolen the signs from a work site the previous night. With Luny's mum's trailer attached to Luny's car, they'd driven to where a road system was being developed for a new housing area. There were signs everywhere and it didn't take long to purloin the four they needed and the brackets which enabled them to be free-standing.

When Luny showed Dek the guns inside his flat, Dek's immediate response was: "They're too long."

The guns were the over-and-under type—one barrel on top of the other—favoured in target shooting.

"How are we going to swing these around quickly? he said. "They don't even look that intimidating! We'll look like a couple of farmers."

Luny bridled. "We don't have much fucking choice. It's not like we can drive down to fucking K-Mart and get a couple of Glocks. Price check aisle five, Glock nine millimetre with fifteen-round mag," he said in his best nasally check-out-person drawl.

"Can't we cut them off? Isn't sawn-off the fashion for violent crimes?"

"Oh sure, my brother would barely notice that you had trimmed eight inches off his eight-thousand dollar competition gun. A gun's a gun, these boys will know what they are when we point them at them, and they'll know what they can do."

Feeling chided, Dek said nothing more on the subject. They loaded the signs into the back of the utes and were ready to head off.

The plan was to drive down along the route that the bikies would take and walk through the strategy.

They would repeat the crucial activities again on Wednesday, the day before the operation.

The drive down also provided an opportunity to test the radios. Luny had gone for the UHF option after a lot of reading and getting annoyed with the pimple-faced shop assistant who, Luny suggested to Dek, didn't know his arse from his elbow when it came to radio frequencies.

Taking the radio communication very seriously, Luny came up with a couple of radio 'handles' so that they could remain largely anonymous. It was agreed that they would say as little as possible about the activities they were undertaking over the open airwaves. They had their phones as back-up.

Driving in tandem for ninety minutes they reached the turn-off onto an unsealed road at a hamlet with a handful of houses. Dek pulled over on the side of the road, and Luny pulled in behind.

"I was thinking that you should wait here and I'll drive on ahead and find a likely spot on the mountain. Then we can time how long it will take for them to get there from here. It'll also give us a chance to see if the radios work from this far out," said Dek.

"Crikey, nice thinking," said Luny, making no attempt to hide his surprise at Dek's pragmatic approach to the operation.

Wending its way up and over small hills, the road took Dek through native eucalyptus bush on one side opening out into fertile basalt grazing country and a couple of distant farmhouses on the other. Even in his task-focused frame of mind Dek was briefly distracted by the bucolic scene thinking it was like an Arthur Streeton painting.

Dek slowed at the outskirts of a tiny village, slightly bigger than the previous place where they had stopped. Nothing much moved as he drove through. A sign near the road alerted motorists that the general store was open for business, but the only sign of life was a wisp of smoke curling from the chimney.

It wasn't until Dek drove past the last house on the edge of the village that he saw another person, a small boy sitting on a bike with training wheels in the front yard of his home. The boy gave a furtive wave as Dek drove past. Dek waved back.

"Copy me Mr. White?" Dek said using the *noms de guerre* they had chosen from Tarantino's *Reservoir Dogs*. It had been the first flippant moment they had shared in many days.

"Loud and clear Mr. Brown."

Dek drove away from the village towards the edge of the escarpment, passing a gravel road on his left. The open grazing land quickly gave way to thick eucalyptus forest where the road dropped away down the mountain. Luny had warned him that they would not have radio contact if he went too far.

After negotiating a couple of bends Dek thought the next corner looked promising. He didn't stop because their was no verge, which was what had attracted him to the spot.

"Copy me Mr. White?" asked Dek, a little further down the road.

"Read you okay Mr. Brown," Luny came back, the signal not nearly as clear as the first transmission, but still audible.

"Ok, drive on towards me and time it," Dek said.

"Roger that."

Parking his ute on the road verge, two hundred metres from the corner he had chosen, Dek settled in to wait for Luny.

"Fourteen-forty-seven," said Luny stepping out of his ute.

They walked back up the road to the corner.

"This looks like a good spot, nice and isolated," said Luny scanning the area. He smiled at Dek, and dipped his head acknowledging his choice.

"Yep, we'll do it here," said Dek with finality. "We'll drop a sign at the turn-off back up the road, and another at the bottom."

They didn't linger, climbing back into their utes, driving to the bottom of the mountain before Dek spoke again on the radio.

"The other sign here I think," he said, as they pulled out of the final bend of the mountain road and onto the long straight stretch that lead towards another small town, a handful of kilometres in front of them.

"Roger that," came the reply.

They continued on through the town towards Merimbula, reaching the house in the early afternoon.

Argo knew that Fist had flown to Sydney by himself the weekend before. He suspected that whatever was going down would happen soon. He'd arranged for his men to work shifts keeping an eye on Fist's movements. He'd hired a couple of different cars to avoid his men being spotted as they parked on the main access road leading to Fist's house.

Argo wanted Fist followed everywhere he went for the next week. His men had already begun to grumble about wasting hours sitting around doing nothing. A quick clip under the ear of one, had quietened the grumbles.

Fist had done nothing out of the ordinary to this

point, spending several hours each day at the two brothels run by the club, and going to the clubhouse in the evenings.

After a couple of days of fruitless effort, Argo got a break from an unlikely quarter. He was talking to his current girlfriend, a woman much younger than he, attracted by the thrill of going out with the leader of a bikie club, a situation not supported by her parents.

Argo discussed very little of the club's business with her but she was aware he was desperately trying to figure out what the Mongrels were up to.

"I meant to tell ya, my mate Trace told me that a big group of bikies were drinking at the pub where she works on Sunday. One of them mentioned he was going to Nowra on Thursday. I'm pretty sure they were Mongrels. She thought this guy was pretty cute…"

"You sure about this?" Argo interrupted. She suddenly had Argo's undivided attention.

"Well that's what she told me."

"Look this is really important, is that what she said? Give her a call and ask her. I wish you'd fuckin' mentioned this on Sunday."

"I didn't realise it was important, you don't tell me much, how am I supposed to know."

"Just fuckin' call her will you, it's really important."

A few minutes later Argo had his confirmation and his mood brightened considerably.

Not unlike Dek and Luny, the ACT police were scurrying to put their operation together. They had gathered a task-force of officers from all three represented forces, and working from the cramped Eden Police Station, planned a comprehensive surveillance operation centred on the wharf cafe.

Sitting with a smugness she could barely contain, Rider didn't make a sound as she perched on the edge of her seat listening to every detail of the plan. The boss had come through for her and she couldn't have been happier.

She'd almost peed herself with the excitement. Holding tight to her pelvic floor muscles, she'd managed to keep her delight hidden behind a poker face, outwardly trying to look as if this kind of situation was part of her daily routine. Inside she was erupting with sparks that sent shivers through her body. This was her big break.

Her excitement was tempered a little when she realised she had been designated the role of look-out along the route the bikies would take to Eden. Her job was to advise when the bikies had passed by, that was all. While she was somewhat annoyed at this trivial role, she was smart enough to keep her views to herself. She was part of an important operation, she was sure more opportunities would follow.

When Dek and Luny arrived at the Merimbula house they were quick to park one of the Toyotas in the garage away from curious eyes that might recall two identical white utes parked together. The other they parked on the street.

The rest of the day was spent running through the plan. As evening rolled around they bought takeaway pizza and a six-pack of Stella—Dek noticed Luny's beer choice but said nothing.

Despite the short timeframe, both men were largely content with their plan. They could see no obvious major flaws, and had fully minimised the risks as much as risk could be minimised, when making life-long enemies of a bikie gang.

The next morning, with one day before the operation, they took one ute back up to Mt Darragh to run through the scenario on the ground. The key to their success was the main roadblock.

Dek had run off another spread sheet that captured a number of potential outcomes, each driven by different scenarios which the bikies might present. The crucial point was getting the bikies to stop.

Once they agreed that all potential outcomes had been analysed and the various roles allocated between them they drove down a nearby fire road so Luny could show Dek how the shotgun worked. They parked in a big clearing surrounded by towering eucalypts.

Dek had little experience with guns, limited to having fired a twenty-two rifle several times on a friend's farm when he was in high school. When Luny handing him the shotgun he held it at arm's length, staring at it with a look of doubt on his face.

"Don't be a wussy," said Luny seeing Dek wince, "my twelve-year-old nephew shoots one of these. Right, the gun is broken, and no, it doesn't mean it won't work, it means it's open. Here, take it from me. Right you've got two barrels, one above the other and both are empty. Here are two cartridges. Slide them in one at a time, now snap the gun closed firmly.

Dek did as he was bid and the gun gave a satisfying click.

"Right," said Luny. "It's loaded and ready to fire, so don't point it this way and keep your finger away from the trigger until I tell you. You'll see in front of the trigger guard you've got a safety switch, which pushes one way or the other. When it shows red, it's ready to fire. When it shows black, you can't fire it."

Luny walked in closer to Dek, pointing towards the business area of the gun.

"You'll see that you only have one trigger. Some guns have two, one to fire each barrel. These guns have one that fires both barrels. You pull it once and then pull it again. I've set both guns to fire the top barrel first. I'll tell you why I've done that in a minute."

Luny was all business and very professional. His obvious knowledge helped Dek to relax a little, and the more Luny explained, the more his racing heart beat slowed to a more reasonable pace.

Grabbing a couple of soft drink cans he had brought along, Luny placed them twenty metres away.

"Pull the butt of the gun into your shoulder, firmly but not too tight," he said nodding to Dek to do so, " Now sight along the barrel with with your right eye."

"Should I shut my left eye?" asked Dek, squinting along the barrel.

"No, not if you can help it. You don't want to lose your peripheral vision. Now aim at one of the cans and squeeze the trigger. Keep it firm on your shoulder and you won't have a problem."

The only thing Dek could hear was his heartbeat pounding in his ears. There was nothing else at that point just him and the gun in his hands. Even the can on the ground that he was aiming at had ceased to play a role. He tried to slow his breathing. He wanted to make a good show of this for Luny's sake.

He started to squeeze gently on the trigger. The anticipation was excruciating. When he felt the trigger click, he farted, a millisecond before the gun boomed and belched its lethal load.

Dek was more surprised than Luny when the can jumped away from him.

Dek turned towards Luny with a big grin on his face.

"Don't fucking turn towards me, the gun's still loaded and ready to fire, and I don't care if the safety is on. You either fire both shots or open the gun. Got it?"

"Got it," said Dek, his initial excitement squashed under Luny's onslaught.

Dek turned back and fired the second barrel, hitting the other can.

"That was much easier than I thought."

"Here, take some cartridges. Let's see you load it and fire it a couple of times."

Luny had to admit that Dek had taken to the process fairly quickly and was happy to see he was getting comfortable with the weapon.

"Right, before you reload, you remember I said the top barrel fires first, well I thought we should load the top barrel with rock salt. Rock salt is basically some big chunks of salt, that I've loaded into a few cartridges."

Luny pulled a cartridge out of his pocket.

"Looks no different to the others. If I fired one at you at around ten metres or more it would sting like shit, bruise you, and draw some blood on bare skin but would be unlikely to kill you. If I aimed for the eyes it might blind you but otherwise it's only going to inflict superficial wounds and some pain."

"I was thinking we would load the top barrels with rock salt, and at the first sign of aggression from the bikies, we let them have it, no hesitation. Your second barrel will have normal shot in it."

"I'd forgotten why we we're here for a second," said Dek, "it's starting to get a bit scary."

"If they reach for a gun we'll have to go hard," said Luny, not wanting to say what that meant. "Have a few more shots, practice reloading. If you need more than two shots you'll need to be able to get the cartridges in quickly and smoothly."

Dek fired off another dozen or so shots.

"I think that will do us, we'd better get out of here before we attract anyone's attention," said Luny.

Luny cleaned both guns once they got to the house.

"Let's go and have some lunch down town and then come back and run through the details one final time," he said packing the guns away.

When they returned to the house after lunch, both men were very quiet as they sat in front of the television. Dek was first to speak.

"It's not too late to pull out of this...we won't have lost much, a few dollars. It's been an adventure to this point, maybe that's enough."

Luny didn't say anything for a bit.

"Yeah, I was thinking the same thing," he said running his fingers through his hair and scratching the back of his head. "I was feeling cocky these last couple days but now it's become very real and it scares the shit out of me. Let's sleep on it and talk again in the morning. If one of us says 'no' we don't go, no questions asked, ok?"

"Ok," said Dek, knowing that what they were doing would change his life one way or the other.

Neither slept very well that night.

Meeting in the kitchen the next morning, they looked at each other, Dek nodded and Luny did the same. Nothing more was said between them on the matter.

10

Fist didn't sleep very well either, getting out of bed quietly on Thursday morning before five o'clock. He tiptoed out of the bedroom not wanting to wake his wife who was eight months' pregnant.

He put the jug on and dropped a Lipton teabag into a chipped mug and sat down at the kitchen table. He was a little concerned about the plan for today but couldn't think of anything specific that he might not have considered.

He had spoken with a few of the big boys in Sydney and they seemed relaxed about his plan. He had a good reputation, he knew that, but he also knew that it was all business and any mistake with this much cash or product would not bode well for him.

Given it was not the weekend, Fist thought that

it would make spotting a tail easier with fewer cars likely to be on the road. Fist wasn't particularly worried whether or not he spotted a tail, just as long as they were following him, and not the other guys riding to Eden.

He was comfortable that the boys he was sending to Eden were reliable. Turd had been with him for a few years and he was happy to place a bit trust in him. Fist had seen him in a few tough situations and he seemed to make good decisions under pressure, he'd hopefully keep the others in line and get the job done. Fist hoped he was over-worrying the situation.

Having woken early as well, Argo was amped for a big day that might end with him having murdered someone. Far from worrying him, the idea of killing got his blood pumping. Anticipation heightened his senses and he loved the buzz.

Argo had a man placed near Fist's house who would call as soon as Fist moved anywhere. His crew had slept at his house, and were ready to get into the hire car and leave at a moment's notice.

It was around nine when Argo got the call that three of the Mongrels had arrived in a white Falcon, and were currently at Fist's house. Argo got his boys into the car—the weapons were already covered over on the floor of the rear seat—and drove in the direction of Fist's house.

When they were a short distance away, the phone rang again. The man told Argo the Mongrels were on the move heading towards Queanbeyan.

"Foot down, we gotta move," said Argo to his driver.

They caught the tailing vehicle in a few minutes. Argo called his man in the other car and told him that he would take over and that he was to return his hire car.

Given that he had no idea how the buy was to happen Argo figured he and his boys would have to wing it. He didn't have a plan, he was running on instinct. But he really hoped he had an opportunity to teach his supplier and Fist a lesson. With a bit of luck, Argo thought, he would be driving home with some gear and a pile of cash.

Only three of the four riders designated by Fist for the Eden buy left Canberra on schedule. Snuts' machine started running rough as soon as he left his house. He didn't want to get caught on the side of the road with a gun in his saddle-bag half-way to Eden. He called Turd hoping he hadn't already left.

"Fuck, that's fuckin' great," was Turd's opening

gambit. "Alright, there's nothing we can do now, we need to get going. Give Spanner a call and see if he can do anything quickly. Fist isn't going to be happy. Fuck!"

"Should I call Fist?" asked Snuts.

"No, no don't call him. There's no time to do anything else now. Just give Spanner a call and leave it with me."

Turd was nervous enough about the operation without Fist yelling down the phone at him. He knew the three of them could get the job done, so he made a decision and avoided the call to Fist.

Headed out onto the highway towards Cooma, Turd, knowing that the other two blokes were not far ahead of him felt the churn in his stomach starting to ease. Winding the big Harley up to the speed limit, he settled in the seat. He loved nothing more than cruising.

Less than an hour later, he reached the outskirts of Cooma, slowing for the left hand turn that would take him through the industrial area of the town. He backed off at the rough railway crossing and then gave the throttle a tweak, roaring through the lower gears to get back up to speed, a smile flitted across his face.

The truck stop was not far ahead and he could

already see the other two men parked at the front sitting astride their machines. He pulled in beside them and shut off the engine.

"Snuts' bike's playing up. We need to go without him. Let's do it."

Turd forestalled any response from the other two by firing up his machine and heading off. They rode in line for another twenty minutes, slowing as they reached the small town of Nimitabel.

Turd glanced at the pie shop on other side of street, a couple of cars already out the front, the occupants no doubt enjoying the fair. The early morning twist in his guts hadn't allowed him to eat any breakfast but he thought now he could go a couple of steak and bacon pies to fill the hole. As much as he wanted those pies, he knew better than to stop and risk being late to Eden.

The police look-out in Cooma, parked in an unmarked car outside a steel fabrication business down the road from the truck stop, called the boss to say that only three bikes had passed through, and were now heading down the highway.

The next lookout was the local cop from the small town the bikies reached thirty minutes later. His task was to alert the boss when the bikes had passed through town, and to follow them and make sure they took the next few turns as the bikies had planned. The boss made it very clear that he was not to follow them once they turned onto the gravel road at the small hamlet, the view being, the bikies might be watching for a tail.

Once the bikes had passed him by, the cop, sitting in his own, unmarked, car starting reversing out from his park to follow. He was halfway through the manoeuvre when a long blast from a car horn forced him to brake suddenly. He looked to his left and realised that the white ute beside him had chosen the same moment to begin reversing. He had enough space to drive forward and pull out onto the highway ahead of the ute, ignoring the driver's protestations.

The next check-point belonged to Octavia Rider.

She was sitting restlessly in her unmarked Falcon in front of the General Store in a small rural town, awaiting her turn. She jumped when her mobile rang.

"Hey," Plumber was all business, unlike the previous night. "They're heading your way, about half an hour. Follow, but stay well back you hear?"

"Thanks boss, got it." Plumber broke the connection.

Stomach flutters were a common theme on that morning in that neck of the woods.

Rider had arrived in the town over an hour before the bikes were due to pass through. She was thankful that the store was open and was able to grab a coffee, having missed breakfast that morning. And while stomach flutters were a factor in her missing breakfast, it was as much due to her need to sneak back from Plumber's room to shower and change before the final briefing.

Rider was used to interest from men. What she hadn't seen coming in the bar the night before, and found surprising, was this time it was from her boss. Like most decisions she made, she considered the potential ramifications of a liaison with Plumber very carefully before acting. Given his seniority in the ACT Police she could see only benefit to a relationship, one-off or otherwise, particularly as she knew he was married with kids.

"Looks like there's only three of them," Luny said as he drove out of Nimitabel, his mobile on speaker and his voice tight in his throat. "I nearly had a fucking prang with some idiot in the main street who tried to back into me."

"Everything ok?"

"Yeah, all good now, the bikes are just ahead, along

with the moron who tried to drive into me. As I said, there's only three bikes not four."

"Ok, I'll hear from you shortly."

"Ok," said Luny breaking the connection.

Luny called Dek again ten minutes later.

"Alright, they've turned onto the Bombala Road. Hopefully the next time you hear from me it will be on the radio."

Luny switched on the radio handset, checking it was on the agreed channel. He increased his speed a little, and eased off again when he had the bikies in sight five or six hundred metres ahead of him. The car he'd almost collided with in Nimitabel had also turned onto the Bombala Road, and was between him and the bikes.

As Luny approached the hamlet he could see the bikes take the left-hand turn onto the gravel road. The car ahead of him continued straight towards Bombala. He tried the radio.

"Mr. White, do you copy, over?"

"Loud and clear, Mr. Brown, loud and clear," Dek fired back.

Luny let out a big sigh of relief. While they had tested the radios on their way to Merimbula, and they had worked well, he knew that changing weather conditions and other variables could affect the signal strength. He did not want to rely on mobile phones.

"Just passed checkpoint one, turn made," said Luny.

"Roger that," said Dek. Feeling a little rise of his heartbeat with the acknowledgment this was the signal for him to put out the road-closed sign at the bottom of the mountain, and move up to the corner they had chosen.

"No cars ahead," Dek added, which meant that no one had passed him in the time he had been on the mountain road. It reduced the likelihood that there would be any traffic between him and Luny.

Luny's stomach, already knotted with tension, began turning somersaults. He followed the bikes onto the gravel road that he and Luny had driven along a couple of days before. Putting more pressure on the accelerator he started to gain on the Harleys, and realised that the big, heavy machines would not be at home on the slippery gravel surface and corrugated corners. He checked his speed to ensure he did not close the gap too much but was close enough to see the sun glinting off the bikes chromework.

Luny followed the bikies up and over the rolling hills topping the final rise before the run down into the town which the bikies were just entering.

"Checkpoint two reached," he said into his radio.

"Roger that. I'm in position," said Dek. It was his signal to Luny that he was at the top of the mountain with the road-closed sign in position at the first bend.

Luny entered the town, turning back onto a bitumen surface in the main street. He could see, as well as hear the bikes accelerating as they reached the hundred kilometre speed sign at the edge of town. As he drove out of town a little boy sitting on his bike in the front yard of a house waved to him.

Luny snorted a laugh. The little boy had broken the spell that had bound Luny to the task at hand. Giving the boy a vigorous wave Luny laughed again shaking his head at the absurdity of the situation in which he found himself.

A short distance from town he came to a junction where a gravel road joined the mountain road. Slamming on the brakes, Luny jumped from his car and pulled the road signs from the back of the ute. Pushing them into the stirrups, he felt his heart quicken with the impact of what he was doing. This is it, he thought, no going back now.

Leaping into the ute, slamming the door, he took off, screeching the tyres, revving the engine to its red-line in each gear as he raced to catch up to the bikes before they reached the road block. He caught sight of the them just as they entered the first tight curve, that signified the beginning of the mountain descent.

The crucial moment was two corners ahead. What would the bikies do when they saw the road block he wondered? With the sign placed out of sight around a reasonably tight bend, Dek and Luny hoped the bikies would have no time to turn before reaching the road block. All their preparation hinged on the bikies stopping without suspicion, for a few moments at least.

Luny had closed the distance to within fifty metres of the bikes and saw the brake lights as they rounded the final bend and were confronted with Dek's road block. Turning the corner, Luny got closer and saw the flasher spinning. Bright, stark, business-like lights, on top of Dek's ute was the first thing to catch his eye.

Dek stood beside the ute looking anything but convincing. He was wearing orange overalls, a white hard hat and a pair of Cancer Council sunglasses that managed to cover most of the face. He was wearing the same outfit as Luny. But all Luny saw was a tall skinny man looking very out of place, standing like he was at attention. He hoped that it was enough to fool the bikies and make them stop.

Dek had completely blocked the road with his sign and his ute, providing no option for the Harleys but to stop or turn around.

With shaking hands hands, Luny stopped the ute a short distance behind the bikes. His face burned as his over-stimulated nervous system flooded its vessels with blood. His chest felt like a Japanese drummer was hammering away on the inside. He jumped out, pulling the shotgun from its blanket in the back. The Harley engines were still running.

Turd rounded the bend and was forced to brake hard as he saw the road blocked a short distance in front of him. He hoped the other bikes had seen it as well and would not run up his arse. His anger flared. What fucking idiot would put a road-block half-way through a blind corner with no warning signs.

This last thought turned his anger to suspicion, particularly when the bloke in the orange overalls stayed near the back of his ute instead of coming forward to talk to him. Turd didn't like the feel of it.

"Let's go," he mouthed to the other two, jerking his head backwards to indicate the direction from which they had come.

He had pulled up close to the centre line, the other two bikes on his outside. The road was cambered towards the inside of the corner and he let the big machine roll that way. Fuck, he knew he wouldn't make the turn in one go and would have to step the heavy bitch backwards. He felt very fucking vulnerable.

He had just given himself enough room when he saw another bloke in orange overalls coming towards him from a ute that had come up behind them. His heart jumped. The guy was carrying a shotgun.

The bloke pointed it at his chest and yelled at him to turn the bike off. Turd didn't hesitate twisting the throttle and dumping the clutch. The Harley let out a bellow and shot forwards, back up the mountain road. The shot took him high in the chest, he barely heard it over the racket of his bike. It hit like a sledge hammer.

The force jerked his hands off his bars. Tumbling backwards, legs over his head, he somersaulted, landing on the rough pebbles and grass of the watercourse on the inside of the road.

The Harley crashed to the bitumen onto on its right side, forcing Luny to jump sideways to avoid it. The engine continued to bellow in protest as the throttle jammed against the road surface, the back wheel spinning crazily.

The other two bikies looked at each other, unsure what to do.

"Kill the engines," yelled Deck, who had grabbed his shotgun and walked towards them.

When they saw Dek was armed as well, they switched the machines off and raised their arms.

Snapping the gun open, Luny was quick to reload the chamber, replacing the spent rock-salt cartridge with a fresh one, striding towards Turd as he did it. He shut the gun and pointed its twin black eyes into Turd's face.

Turd moaned. His chest burned. "This is it," he thought, "I'm fucked." He had rolled onto his back hoping it would lessen the agony.

He eased himself onto his elbows plucking up the courage to look down, expecting to see his guts hanging out. His head shot back in surprise when he saw no entrails nor even any blood. The only obvious wounds were from pellets which had hit him in either cheek releasing two neat runnels of blood down across his face to drip from his chin. He looked like an evil clown.

"That was rock-salt fucker," yelled Luny above the noise of Turd's bellowing Harley. "The next one won't be so friendly." Luny prodded the barrels into

Turd's cheek leaving a neat figure eight in the blood. "Next prick that does something stupid, dies."

Walking backwards Luny kept his gun trained on Turd. Bending down he turned the key on Turd's bike. The noise took a few seconds to abate as the crazed rear wheel slowed, the exhaust coughing at the last as the engine's compression finally overpowered the wheel's forward momentum.

For a brief moment the only sound was the lazy drawl from a crow passing overhead.

Clutching his chest, Turd thought about his gun, a Glock 22 with a fifteen-round magazine. Ironically, it was the same as that favoured by many of Australia's police forces.

Unfortunately, like the other two guys, his gun was wrapped in a cloth in the bottom of his saddlebag, hidden, in case they were pulled over by the cops. The plan had been to retrieve the guns just before they reached the buy.

"Right, off the bikes you two," said Luny, turning towards the other two bikies, "on your knees near this prick, backs to me, hands behind your back and palms together, ankles crossed."

They had rehearsed this. Dek had Googled the standard operating procedures from various police agencies around the world in relation to restraining offenders.

Dek walked to the front of the three kneeling men training his weapon on them. Luny put his gun down and pulled a bag of zip ties from his pocket. He wasted no time trussing each man's hands, and then their ankles, finally joining the two ties with a third. To finish, he pulled beanies over their heads, covering their faces.

Where he thought he would feel fear, Dek only sensed a growing euphoria. He walked behind the three men, prodding each of them roughly between the shoulder blades with the barrel of his gun. The men had to fight to avoid pitching forward onto their faces.

Luny moved towards Turd's bike and opened the saddle bag that was not trapped by the fallen machine.

Turd could hear the buckles being opened. With the realisation that his wounds were not life-threatening he began to focus on what was happening.

"Have you fuckers got any idea what you're doing. You'll die for this."

"Want another rock-salt?" asked Dek.

"Don't you…," was all Turd managed to say before Dek pulled the trigger.

Dek was very close to Turd when he fired the shot, hitting the bikie between the shoulder blades.

The force flung Turd forward. With no way of stopping his face smacking into the bitumen, Turd turned his head at the last moment, his cheek-bone cracking, loud enough to be heard, as it collided with the rough surface. Turd felt the ripping pain as a couple of teeth sheared off at the gum, tearing a big gouge from the inside of his cheek.

"Fuckers," he groaned, lying with his helmeted head on the ground again, spitting the teeth out along with with the blood and tears that had begun filling his mouth.

Luny jumped at the boom of Dek's shot, turning, horrified when he saw Dek's wide eyes and his face lit up in a full-teeth grin.

Luny was shocked but left him to it, going back to his rummaging.

While Turd writhed on the ground, the other two bikies stayed very quiet.

A pssst from Luny made Dek turn. Dek had taken a small Spongebob backpack from the saddle bag. Luny beckoned him to come and help lift the bike so Luny could get to the other saddle bag.

They heaved Turd's Harley upright setting it on

the side stand. Luny pulled an identical backpack from the other saddlebag.

A search of the other two bikes revealed nothing further. A quick look inside one the backpacks showed they had what they were after.

Snuts pulled his machine to a stop at the road-closed-detour sign just outside the small town, peering at the sign and then the road, leaving him perplexed.

After the others had gone he had taken his bike over to Spanner's place who had quickly found the problem, loose nuts on the exhaust mounts. It was a simple fix, with a judicious application of torque wrench getting the bike running smoothly in minutes.

He was only twenty minutes behind the others. Rather than face Fist's wrath he decided to follow them, riding fast, with a view to catching up with them long before Eden.

When he reached the road-closed sign, he was puzzled. If they had turned around he would have met them. He turned briefly down the gravel side road looking for motorcycle tyre marks in the loose gravel. He couldn't see any marks. He turned back, rode around the signs, and headed down the mountain road.

Dek and Luny dragged the last of the bikies over the road edge and down into the ferns, depositing him beside the others.

Stepping back Dek dealt the man a resounding kick in the stomach, letting out a nervous chuckle as he paced back looking at them all trussed and hooded in the anti-foetal position. The Harleys lay in a tangled heap nearby.

Luny grabbed Dek by the arm, a frown on his face, and pulled Dek towards the road. As Luny began to climb up the bank, Dek, still carrying his gun, walked back to the pile of Harley's and fired a shot. The rocksalt gouged paint from the tank of the nearest machine, leaving a dent and defacing the air-brushed black skull motif.

"Fuck, what are you doing," yelled Luny, breaking the minimal-speaking rule they had agreed on.

Dek shrugged and ran up the bank.

As they crested the road edge they both stopped. There was no mistaking the sound of a Harley Davidson in the distance.

"It must be the fourth one," said Luny, "let's go."

Luny sprinted up the road to his ute, roaring off in pursuit of Dek, down the mountain road.

11

Snuts rounded the bend to see the road-closed sign in front of him. He eased off the throttle looking to pass the sign on the inside of the curve. With the Harley idling past the sign he did a double-take when he heard his name yelled.

He pulled to a halt just past the sign switching off his machine.

"That's fucking Turd's voice," he said aloud.

He kicked down the side stand and ran back up the road peering into the bush to see a tangle of Harleys, before hearing a bellow from Turd nearby.

"Hurry up, fuck you, cut me loose," yelled Turd from beneath his hood.

Snuts blanched when he pulled the beanie from Turd's head. His nose and mouth were a bloody mess.

Both lips were split and his nose was skinned and bent at a funny angle and when he spoke Snuts could see the gaping hole where some of his teeth used to be.

Turd pulled out his safety blade and cut the ties from Turd's hands and ankles.

"Someone's got the cash, I'm taking your bike." Snuts had barely understood the statement made with a strong lisp. "Get these bikes out and follow as soon as you can. I'll call when I can and tell you where to go."

Turd ran to his bike, grabbed the Glock from the saddle bag, ran up the bank and leaped onto Snuts' machine, tearing off after the utes as fast as he could ride.

"You hear me," said Luny into the radio.

"Yep, got you."

"We need to go fast," said Luny.

"Yep."

"But careful on the bends, these things will tip."

Dek pushed the ute through the tight curves of the mountain road as fast as he dared. The utes were not designed for cornering and accelerating. They were work trucks with off-road capability. They were tall and top heavy. Luny drew his breath through clenched teeth on a couple of occasions as he followed Dek through the corners.

On what turned out to be the final bend of the descent Luny rounded the corner on Dek's tail. Dek swerved all of a sudden to avoid the sign he had left there. Luny swore and veered clipping the mirror on the driver's side and smashing it from his bracket.

"Fuck," he said. He didn't bother chastising Dek for the lack of a warning.

Once they had crossed the small bridge at the bottom of the descent it was a straight run to the the next town, five kilometres away. They were still a kilometre or so out when Luny saw a motorcycle in the distance in his mirror, closing the gap without much effort.

"Fuck, he's almost caught us," said Luny into his radio. "But we don't know if he's chasing us or not."

"We need to be sure," said Dek. "When we get through town there's a turn-off to the left, a kilometre past the town, you go straight ahead and I'll turn. There's another left about a kilometre further on, called Badger Hole Road, you turn there."

"If he follows you, we'll know. That road comes out on the road I'm taking. I'll take it from the other end. Stay on the radio, we should meet after a couple of kilometres and be able to surprise him. Did you catch all that?"

"I think so, Badger Road a few kilometres past town," said Luny.

"That'll do, don't miss that turn. Good luck."

They hit the small town doing one-hundred-and-forty, the utes not capable of much greater speed. Dek slowed for the slight bend in the main street, just past the general store.

Luny checked his mirror and saw that the Harley was only about half a kilometre behind them.

Rider was concerned. By her reckoning the bikes should have been there by now.

She picked up her mobile phone and was on the verge of calling the boss when two white utes drove through town way beyond the speed limit.

She didn't concern herself with the situation until a Harley Davidson screamed through town twenty seconds later going even faster. Rider didn't hesitate, she started her unmarked Falcon and took off at speed in pursuit of the bike.

"Yep?" said the boss on the other end of the phone.

"Boss, two utes just tore through here with a Harley hot on their heals. Something has happened. I'm in pursuit but haven't got a visual."

"Shit, righto, try and get a visual but stay back, stay on the line and talk to me. Don't fuck this up."

Rider was excited, she was back in the game. She had the Falcon roaring as she left Wyndham up and over the rise at the edge of town. She passed a turn-off on the left catching a glimpse of the motorcycle on the road ahead of her in the distance.

"Boss," she said, her phone on speaker. "I've got the bike ahead of me, about a kilo."

"Alright, don't get too close but stay in contact. Remember your training."

The road stretched away from her in a straight line for several kilometres. The bike's brake light lit up and then the bike disappeared.

Rider kept her foot to the floor but then slammed on the brakes, locking the wheels as she reached a turn-off to the left. This was about where she had seen the brake lights. The road was gravel and there were fresh slide marks. Rider took the punt.

"Boss," she said, "looks like they've turned onto a dirt road called Big Badger Road, left, off the coast road about two kilometres south of the town, I'm going to follow."

"Fuck," said Plumber, sensing the operation was going pear-shaped. "Alright, stay with them if you can, if they've turned, something has happened. At least we can try and grab the bikie. Be careful, he's probably armed. Make sure you…" Rider had swept over a ridge into thick forest, the phone had dropped out.

On a road many kilometres to the north, Fist was doing things at a much less frenetic pace. He had caught sight of a white car a couple of times in his mirror but couldn't be sure he was being tailed. He was tempted to pull over and let it go past to see who was at the wheel, but thought he should stick to the plan and keep the charade going until he reached his destination.

Dek, never much of a driver, surprised himself when he cut the corner at the turn-off, barely lifting his foot from the accelerator. The inside of the intersection was used by the local council to stockpile blue metal for road re-resealing. It was a clear run across the corner. The ute bounced and bucked but stayed upright finding purchase onto the side road.

Luny kept his foot down charging past the turn-off and breathing a sigh of relief when Dek successfully navigated the turn. He turned his focus back to his mirror to see the Harley closing on him quickly.

It was almost on his tail when he saw the turnoff to

Big Badger Road. A final glance in the mirror before the turn was enough to know he was being followed. The face in his mirror, even from that distance, was unmistakable, largely because of the busted lips, nose and teeth and the quantity of drying blood.

Luny braked hard, swinging the ute violently off the sealed surface onto the gravel road. The rear end fishtailed, wheels spinning in the gravel, flicking rocks into the air as he slid over the loose shale. Holding on tight to the steering wheel, Luny fought to get it under control. He flicked the range selector into HIGH 4 mode increasing his traction on the slippery surface.

He looked into his mirror again to see the Harley falling away a little behind him.

"You hear me?" said Luny into the radio, wrestling the Hilux one-handed.

"Got you."

"He's followed me onto the gravel road. We're heading your way. It's the one we shot," said Luny, immediately regretting saying this last part over the open radio system.

"Ok," said Dek. "I should be on you in a couple of minutes. Speed up a little and make him go a bit faster, and stay left."

Luny was already on the edge of control but put his

foot down even more, the ute bucking around and feeling loose in the rear wheels.

Turd had ridden like a valkyrie down the mountain, reefing on the bars and scraping the foot pegs on most of the corners, pushing the big machine as fast as he dared. He had hit well over two hundred kilometres an hour on the long run towards town and had taken the bend in the main street at one hundred and sixty.

By the time he left town he was close to catching the utes. When one split off onto a side road he ignored it and kept on ahead to pursue the other. He had to brake hard at another turn-off when the ute veered suddenly onto another gravel road. He wanted to call the boys but dared not stop.

He rode as fast as he could to try and stay with the ute on the slippery surface, but it was a losing battle as he wrestled with a machine, not his own, and designed for highway cruising. He winced in pain, from the rock-salt rounds fired at him, catching his breath each time the Harley hit a bump. He almost dropped the heavy machine on one corner when he caught the front wheel in a ridge of loose gravel running up the centre of the road. He slowed to gain control falling further behind the ute.

Fuck, thought Turd. We'd better get to a sealed road soon or I'm fucked.

The road straightened briefly into a gentle left-hand bend over a rise. Turd twisted the throttle open to try and take back some lost ground. As he crested the rise, focused on keeping the Harley upright on the loose surface, he did not see the second ute coming straight at him until it was practically on top of him. With his impetus on the corner already taking him to the right-hand side of the ride he had no choice but to steer off into the bush to avoid a head-on collision.

The big bike left the road and flew through the air, Turd clinging gamely to the bars. Time slowed. It was almost peaceful, serene even, thought Turd, until an eighty year old Yellow Box Eucalyptus interrupted his flight.

The front wheel hit square, buckling under the impact, pushing the forks back against the engine housing. Turd was flung off the side like a rag doll, missing the tree by inches. He landed in the bush on a pile of long-ago fallen leaf litter and bark, touching down like a glider, bouncing up and then back down again, before tumbling end over end, coming to a halt in a dusty clearing.

He lay quietly for a moment in the bush, gradually moving his limbs one-by-one to ascertain some extent of his injuries and pondering his good fortune once again when discovering he seemed in reasonable health, all things considered.

He reached for his Glock which had survived the ordeal in the waistband of his jeans in the small of his back. He pulled the gun out and clicked off the safety, struggling to his knees, moaning briefly from the clutching pain in his chest and his back.

Luny and Dek had stopped together where Turd had left the road, pondering their next move. They could just make out the bent and busted Harley lying in the bush, but of the pilot there was no sign.

"We'd better check him," said Dek.

"And what if he's still alive? What if he's armed, what are we going to do with him?" demanded Luny.

"Will he get a phone signal here?" asked Dek.

"Nothing on mine," said Luny, checking his phone. "Let's leave him. He can't call them on to us and he hasn't seen our faces. Let's get going in case the others are heading this way."

"Alright, follow me, I'll take a few back roads around in case they're looking for us."

They climbed back into the utes and headed the way Dek had come.

Rider arrived about a minute after Dek and Luny had

departed, slamming on her brakes when she saw the skid marks where the Harley had left the road. She jumped out to peer into the bush. It didn't take her long to see the twisted wreck of the Harley. She slid down the steep bank and headed towards it, drawing her gun.

As she neared the bike a voice demanded from her left: "Who the fuck are you?"

"I'm a cop," said Rider turning towards the voice, starting at the sight of the bloodied and battered Turd, his gun pointed in her direction.

Rider's first instinct was a good one, stepping slightly to her left, putting a young tree between her and the bikie. Turd fired, a chunk of bark flying off the side of the tree.

Rider dived for the cover of a larger tree, several shots zinging past her. She stood up with her back to the huge trunk. The bikie had stopped shooting, she could hear him moving through the undergrowth. Raising her gun in both hands, as she had been taught, she stepped to the side of the tree, her finger taking up the slack on the trigger, her arms extending. The bikie was nowhere in sight and she could no longer hear him moving.

Her breathing was shallow and rapid and didn't help her as she tried to listen. She forced herself to take a couple of deeper breaths. She checked her phone but had no signal.

When Rider had dived behind the tree, Turd had moved to his left, holding his breath against the burn coursing through his battered chest, which had taken the first shot on top of the mountain, and then been the contact point for his flying dismount from the Harley.

He ducked behind a tree, releasing his breath slowly, wincing at the clutching pain. He saw the cop sneak a peak from behind her tree, about thirty metres away. She had looked the wrong way and not seen him. He realised he held the advantage, for now.

He needed to get a clearer shot, so moved further to his right, attempting to get behind Rider. He took small, careful steps, doing his best to avoid treading on dead branches, a sound which would betray his position.

He was now almost directly behind Rider, between her and her car. He wondered whether she would have left her keys in the ignition.

Turd wasn't sure what to do. He didn't want to kill a cop but now that he had shot at her, he would go away for a long time when they caught him. She was the only one who had seen him. He realised he needed to finish the job and get out before anyone else turned up.

Turd moved out from his cover. He could see Rider crouching behind her tree. He took a bead and squeezed the trigger. The shot was loud in the quiet that had settled in the forest. Rider screamed and fell forward, the shot taking her in the left shoulder. She turned on her stomach, firing wildly in the direction she thought the shot had come from. She still couldn't see Turd.

Turd had moved further to his right and was now closer to Rider than before. He stepped from behind a towering eucalyptus and fired again. The shot hit Rider in the head.

"Sorry pig, not your lucky day," said Turd, as he approached, his gun still pointing at Rider. Only when he saw the blood from her head wound did he lower his weapon. He searched her pockets for keys, but finding none set off towards her car.

He pushed back through the bush towards the road, wincing at every step and struggling to take a deep breath. Turd figured he had at least a couple of broken ribs. He climbed slowly up the bank to the road edge.

"Thank fuck," he said aloud as he looked through

the window of the car and saw the key in the ignition.

He climbed gingerly in, sweat rolling down his back and face from the effort and the pain.

He reached for his phone but had no signal. He tossed it onto the seat, started the car and drove off in the direction taken by the utes.

When he reached a t-intersection, a sealed road in front of him, he checked his phone again to find he now had a signal.

The other bikies had succeeded in pulling their machines back up onto the road and were passing through the small town where Rider had been waiting. When they got to the turn-off that Dek had taken, they stopped. Snuts got his phone out and was about to call Turd, when his phone rang.

"It's me," said Turd, "where are you?"

"At the turn-off to Candelo."

"Take the turn-off. I'm in a blue Falcon a couple of kilometres along, hurry," yelled Turd, before hanging up, forestalling any further discussion.

They met Turd on the side of the road a couple of minutes later.

"Where did you get the wheels?" asked one.

"Where's my bike?" Snuts looked crestfallen.

"Never fucking mind. Shut up and listen. If you didn't see those utes, it means they've headed back this way. Get after them. Call me as soon as you find them. Don't stop looking, split up if you need to. I need to call Fist and that won't be fucking good. Stop and call me every fifteen minutes. Now go."

The three bikes roared off leaving Turd worried about what he would say to Fist. Shooting a cop was easy compared to ringing Fist and telling him they'd fucked up.

Luny and Dek had made it over the mountain road and were a handful of kilometres short of the small town of Candelo.

"We'll turn right just down here," said Dek into his radio.

"Roger that," came the reply. Both had settled a little following the escape from the bikie. Luny wanted to say something to Dek about his behaviour around the bikies but decided it wasn't quite the right time.

They took the right turn onto a gravel road following it through rolling grazing paddocks. Dek then led Luny through a series of roads both sealed and gravel. Luny had no idea where they were. He didn't much care as long as Dek knew and the bikies didn't.

Dek was confident that no one could be following them now.

When Fist saw that it was Turd calling him his heart skipped a beat.

"What the fuck are you doing calling me at this time," yelled Fist into the phone. "You should be at the buy, what the fuck have you done?"

"We got rolled. Two armed guys in white utes stopped us on the mountain road and got away with the money. I chased them, they ran me off the road into the bush. I wrecked the bike. A cop turned up. I had to top her. I'm in her unmarked car."

"You did what! Fuck, stop fucking telling me this on the fucking phone. Are you looking for the utes?"

"The other three are looking and will call in if they see anything. I'll keep looking as well. I need to get rid of this car. What about the buy?"

"That's fairly fucked isn't it. I'll make some calls. Don't worry about the buy. Just find these fuckers and get rid of that car. I'm heading your way down the coast, I should be there in less than two hours. What a fucking mess, you really fucked this up. Find that money."

12

Detective Plumber was getting worried. No sign of the bikes and no further contact from Rider. Something was badly wrong. He sent cars speeding up the road towards Wyndham and Candelo, all pretence of a covert operation now gone.

The three bikies had split up. Two had gone to Candelo and then split, taking two highway options out of the town, the third had taken the gravel road that Dek and Luny had taken, but a long way behind them.

Turd was flying towards Candelo, knowing that he needed to get rid of the car. Unfortunately he was a little slow in acting on his instincts. When he reached Candelo he tried calling the other three but none of them answered his call. He was parked in the main street near the cafe when two police cars, sirens wailing, screamed into town.

Turd, in no doubt they would be looking for the car he was in, started the engine and performed a screeching u-turn heading out of town. The engine screamed under the high revs. The leading police car had spotted the car Turd was driving and was in pursuit a short distance behind.

By the time Turd reached the Anglican church at the top of the short rise on the way out of town he was already doing a hundred and twenty. The corner turned sharply to the right and Turd hit it with way too much speed, swearing as he reefed on the steering wheel and hitting the brakes in an effort to keep the car on the road.

All he succeeded in doing was sending the car over the road edge in a screeching sideways slide, down the embankment, where it rolled several times before coming to a rest on its roof against the fence of a house beside the river.

Turd had not had a good day. Rock-salt to the chest, rock-salt to the back, a flying dismount from Snuts' Harley and now this. He hadn't worn a seat belt and he now lay with the roof of the car underneath him in a growing pool of blood pouring from a gash to his forehead.

Unfortunately for Turd the Glock pistol was lying next to him and he picked it up before crawling through the smashed driver-side window, his eyes filling with blood from his head wound. Two policemen from the lead vehicle were down the bank near his car with weapons drawn. Turd came to his knees turning towards the cops as they yelled at him to drop the gun.

He didn't. They shot him many times.

Dek and Luny were oblivious to what was happening in their wake. Luny could see a t-intersection ahead of them where the gravel road they were on, met a highway.

"I think we should go right here and up the coast road," said Dek into his radio as he slowed for the t-intersection. "It's much further but what if others are on the way from Canberra?"

"Yeah, I thought the same thing," was Luny's response. "We'd better get some fuel though, I don't think I've got enough to get home."

Dek hadn't looked at the fuel gauge in the mayhem.

"Yeah, me too. Let's try in Cobargo."

Twenty minutes later Dek turned off his engine in front of the fuel pump in the small town. Luny pulled in behind him.

"How are you?" said Luny.

"Surprisingly well, all things considered," said Dek with a grin.

"You seemed to take on a different persona back there."

"Yeah, I was just into my character, that's all," said Dek.

"Not sure I want to meet that guy again."

"Well, we're not home yet, let's just wait to see if he's needed again."

Dek pulled forward and Luny fuelled his ute. They continued up the coast highway.

Fist was seriously angry by this stage and a little bit nervous—the first emotion largely driven by a situation out of his control in tandem with a less-than-satisfactory exchange with the supplier, and the second emotion a consequence of his call to Sydney.

But ever-the-professional Fist turned his mind to finding a solution for the problem at hand, getting the cash back.

"Where is that fucking Turd prick?" Fist said

slamming his phone down on the dash of the car. They were near a small town heading down the coast road towards Bega. Fist needed to talk to Turd, to know where to go. He called again. A voice answered, it didn't sound like Turd.

"Who the fuck is this?" was Fist's opening gambit.

The detective on the other end knew who he was talking to, it had come up on the screen of Turd's phone when it rang.

"Ah, Mr. Ellery I presume. We'd like to have a little chat with you."

He didn't get any further as Fist broke the connection.

"Fuck, the cops have got Turd." He tried Snuts. As luck would have it Snuts was sitting at a highway intersection with his phone out, about to call Turd. His heart skipped a beat when the name Fist flashed across his screen.

"Hey Fist," he said tentatively.

"Where are you and what's going on?"

"I've been riding around by myself but haven't seen the utes. I was just about to call Turd."

"Don't, the cops have him. They'll have all our numbers now from Turd's phone. Call the other two and tell them to ditch their SIM cards, and I mean destroy them and the phones. Get to Bega, all three of you and wait for me. Go to the car park at the cheese factory and don't move 'til I get there. We've just passed through Moruya so... did you see that?" Fist said, the men in the car with him not realising Fist was talking to them.

"Snuts, what did those utes look like?" yelled Fist.

"Both white, Hilux tray backs, flashers on top."

"Fuck me, two of them just went past us heading north, fuckin' stop and turn around," Fist yelled at the driver.

The driver slammed on the brakes, reefing the car around and accelerating back in the opposite direction.

"Get on their arse, let's see what they do."

"Fuck, what's he up to?" demanded Argo as Fist's white Falcon went past in the opposite direction.

The quick turn by Fist's car had caught Argo by surprise. There was not much they could do but to keep driving in the direction they were heading.

"Turn around when he's out of sight, and get after him," said Argo to his driver.

Argo groaned, it had been a long day with plenty of fuck ups. He had no idea what Fist was up to. Argo thought they would do the buy somewhere on the coast near Nowra. Fist had stopped at a cafe in the centre of town and Argo had primed his men for action, guns at the ready. But all Fist had done was have lunch! What the fuck was he up to?

They had seen Fist take a call before jumping back in his car and heading south. Now, they had turned back towards Moruya.

"It didn't look like they knew we were there, they never even gave us a look," said the driver.

"Something's happening," said Argo.

"I reckon we drive home through Araluen," said Luny into his radio. It was the first contact between the two men for almost half an hour.

Dek knew the direction he meant. It was a winding gravel road which followed the Deua River from Moruya to the hamlet of Araluen, famous for its peaches. The road then climbed the steep escarpment, and meandered through farm land, coming out on the highway not far from Canberra.

Feeling much more relaxed by this time, Dek thought Luny might be taking the security thing just a tad far. The alternate route would add almost an hour to the journey.

"Do you really think we need to," replied Dek.

"I'm just worried they might have sent someone down the coast road from home."

Any feeling of comfort withered quickly inside Dek. He'd not thought of that.

"Ok, Araluen it is."

When they reached the roundabout in Moruya, they drove straight instead of turning right to follow the highway through the town.

"Where the fuck could they be going? said Fist, "Ease up a bit and let's wait until we get out of town and drive up close to see if we get a reaction from them."

Argo's driver had Fist's car in sight as they drove into Moruya.

"Let's just sit back and see where they're going," said Argo. "They've gone straight ahead onto the Araluen road, don't know why the fuck they'd be going this way, nothing but peaches and fuck all ahead."

Snuts and the other two bikies arrived in Bega at almost the same time. Two of the gang had linked up on the highway, and the third had arrived from the other direction. It was unfortunate that the pair had been spotted riding into town by an officer parked in an unmarked car, whose sole task had been to report on the arrival of Harley Davidson motorcycles. Word on the radio was worrying. Rider's disappearance and possible demise had them all shifting in their seats wondering what the hell had gone down.

The three bikies pulled into the almost-empty cheese factory car park, stopping in the shade of a tall eucalypt. They had barely switched off their machines when the sound of police sirens could be heard close by.

"What the fuck?" said Snuts, "do we make a run?"

The other two just looked at each other. Before any of them could do anything four police cars blocked the only exit from the car park. The cars slid to a stop with officers jumping out and taking shelter behind their cars with weapons drawn.

"Get the fuck onto the ground, now," one of the cops boomed.

Snuts could sense the dangerous mood and quickly raised his arms, stepping off his bike and lying face down on the ground. The other two quickly followed suit.

As Luny and Dek headed up and over the hill out of Moruya, Luny spotted a white sedan. It had followed them onto the Araluen road and had him feeling uncomfortable, his stomach starting to tighten.

Maybe it's just me feeling edgy, he thought. All the same, his guts gripped in a tight cramp after they cleared the town limits and picked up the Deua River. He could see the car was still with them, but somewhat closer.

"Just keep an eye on that white car," said Luny into his radio.

Dek had seen it as well and was monitoring it in his rear-view mirror.

As soon as they left the township the car closed up on them very quickly.

"Just let it pass us," said Dek, his heart starting to beat a little faster.

"Ok," responded Luny.

Both utes slowed on the windy road giving the car space to pass. The car pulled up beside Dek who was following Luny. Looking across as the car paused beside him, he gagged. They were all wearing leathers with patches.

"They're bikies," he yelled into his radio.

Jamming his foot to the accelerator, Luny braced his arms on the wheel. Watching the back of Luny's ute as it left him behind, Dek wasted no time in picking up his pace.

When Fist looked across into the second ute and saw

the open mouth gape of the driver, he knew he had the fuckers responsible for some of the shit that had gone down. The sudden acceleration of both utes only reinforced it.

"Alright boys, let's shoot some tyres," said Fist. "Get up behind this fucker and give me the shotty."

Leaning out the window, gripping the the sawn-off pump-action twelve gauge in his hands, Fist grinned. He loved fixing problems. The driver brought the much faster Falcon up behind Dek's lumbering Hilux and Fist laughed into the wind.

Dek could see the Falcon coming back up on him. He almost peed himself when to his horror, he could see the passenger in the front seat leaning out of the window with a shotgun pointing at him.

The rear of the cab exploded, "Fucking hell," screeched Dek, shielding his face with a hand as pellets ricocheted in the cabin. Flicking glass fragments from his face he grabbed the radio.

Luny heard the shot, Dek was still following.

"You ok?" yelled Luny.

"Not wounded, but fucking scared."

"There's no use trying to outrun them, there's a camping area just up ahead on the left. Turn in there with me, and park behind me. And get your gun out."

The camping area was a cleared piece of flat land beside the river, mostly bare earth with a few patches of scraggly grass. The access track dropped steeply down off the road. The sudden turn by the two utes was enough to throw off Fist's assault.

Fist's driver, Bundy, slowed at the road edge allowing the utes to pull ahead across to the far side of the clearing.

Leaping from their utes, clutching their guns in tight fists, Dek and Luny squatted behind the rear wheels of their vehicles.

As Fist's Falcon drove down into the clearing, Luny ran his eye along the sight, held the gun steady and fired both barrels towards them. Leaning out Dek sucked in a breath, aimed his barrel and squeezed the trigger, the windscreen of the Falcon exploding the glass into a million shards.

"Get us the fuck up the other way," yelled Fist.

Bundy turned away, spinning the Falcon into a slide, the rear wheels kicking up dust and stones while it clawed for traction on the loose surface. He drove to the opposite end of the campground stopping the car in a pall of dust. The bikies jumped out and crouched behind their vehicle.

Fist fired six or seven rounds from his Glock in quick succession. He could hear some of the shots tinging off the tray of the Hilux. One of his men was firing the shotgun.

"Stop firing," he said to the man, "pointless with that from this range, save the ammo."

Fist was annoyed that he only had two weapons among his men. The bulk of the available arsenal was with Turd and the others. Fist punched the door, annoyed at having seen little need to over-arm themselves when they were not planning on any sort of confrontation that day and now all this shit was happening. All they had was the sawn-off twelve gauge and his Glock.

At this range the sawn-off was useless, the shot pattern spreading wildly, long before reaching the target was ineffective. The Glock was another matter. The problem was ammunition, he only had one spare clip.

Fist shouted towards Dek and Luny.

"Just give us the money and you can get out of here. There's no way out otherwise. You're fucked and you'll die here."

Dek and Luny looked at each other. They both recognised the voice they'd heard over the listening device.

"That's Fist," said Luny.

"I know, I recognise him as well, what are we

going to do?" Dek's face was ashen, his voice trembled.

"We need to try and get out of here quick before they get themselves organised. They can call other people in. Who knows how close they might be."

Luny looked to where the clearing ended behind them.

"I reckon we could get the utes up that bank and back onto the road."

Dek looked to see that the clearing ended then pitched steeply up a dry and rocky bank studded with stunted scrub and long grass.

"That's bloody steep," said Dek.

"It's what these things do, and, it's about our only option."

Fist's voice bellowed from the other end of the clearing. "You've got about two minutes, I've got other blokes on the way. It's now or never."

Fist had tried to call Snuts but got no answer.

"Fuck, the first time that fuckin' idiot has acted quickly in his life," said Fist, realising he had told the men further down the coast to get rid of their phones.

Fist then called Spanner, who along with one other man were the last club members still in Canberra. Fist decided to avoid calling Sydney again at this stage, hoping he could get the cash back and save some face.

"Hey Fist," said Spanner.

"Get on your bike and get over to my place," said Fist, "there's some shells for the Glock and some twelve gauge cartridges in the garage. They're in a bag tied to the back of the work bench. I need you to get here as fast as you can."

Fist quickly explained the situation and where they were.

Huddled with Dek behind the rear wheel of Dek's ute, Luny came to a decision. "I reckon we'll have to give them the cash. Let's throw it out into the middle of the clearing and then jump into the utes and get out of here. If they get the cash they might leave us alone."

"Alright," was all Dek said.

13

Argo's driver jammed on the brakes when he heard the first shots, stopping a short distance before the turn to the campground.

"What the fuck is going on?" screamed Argo.

They could see the two white utes at the far side of the campground but were shielded from Fist's Falcon by a copse of trees.

"I reckon it's a buy gone wrong," said the driver.

"Fuckin' aye right, something's gone wrong. Let's sneak up the road a bit on foot and see what we can see. Every one locked and loaded." Each of them had a weapon, two sawn-offs, a thirty-eight revolver and a Glock. Argo had the Glock.

They climbed from the car and edged their way along the fringe of the bush. The shooting had briefly stopped. Argo waved his men down. The entry road to the campground was only a short distance ahead but more importantly they were now looking down through the bush towards Fist and his men crouching behind the Falcon, their backs facing Argo's group.

Before Argo could decide what to do a voice yelled from the end of the clearing where the two utes were parked.

"Alright, we're going to throw out the cash," Luny yelled towards the other end of the clearing.

Dek had gone to Luny's car to get the two Spongebob back-packs.

"That's the smart thing to do," yelled Fist.

Dek came back with the backpacks.

"Toss them just out in front of us a bit so they're nice and close, but so they can see them, they'll have to wait until we go before they can check them."

Dek stood and threw the bags one at a time.

"Alright," said Luny. "get into your ute."

Dek climbed into the passenger-side door, to stay in cover, and climbed across to the driver's seat. Luny leaned in behind him, "Start it up."

With the engine running Luny leaned across and moved the four-wheel-drive selection lever.

"Right, it's low range four wheel drive. Just keep it

in first. It will be super slow but it's what you need to climb the bank. Wait till I get up before you follow. Give it heaps of revs and don't stop until you hit the road. Don't ease off the accelerator for any reason. Keep it straight up the bank, if you try to drive any other way it'll roll."

Dek nodded but said nothing.

Luny jumped into his car, started the engine and selected low range. Just as he was about to drive into the bush and up the bank all hell broke loose behind him.

Argo watched as a man popped up from behind one of the utes and threw out two bags.

"Pay day," he whispered to his men.

He watched as the men climbed into the white utes. This is the best time to nail that bastard Fist, he thought.

"Righto you blokes, fire when I do."

Argo drew a bead on the back of Fist's head and squeezed the trigger. He had made the mistake of many hunters when firing downhill, by not aiming lower. The shot zinged over Fist's head, smashing the rear window of the Falcon. Fist and his three men all turned when they heard the shot and were met by a hail of gunfire from the road above.

Argo caught Fist in the shoulder with his second shot, rolling Fist around and down to the ground. Bundy, Fist's driver, was hit in the chest and face with pellets from one of the sawn-offs. Another man caught pellets in his legs and stomach, only one of them remained unscathed. All four men managed to scramble around to the other side of the car.

Fist heard the cars moving off from across the clearing.

They were a sorry looking bunch, three of them wounded and only two weapons between them.

Fist had no idea who was shooting at them. He thought it couldn't be the cops, they would have made some sort of announcement or demands by now. He fired off a couple of rounds to ensure the attackers knew he and his men were still alive and armed. His gun clicked empty. He reloaded with his final clip. He looked at his men. One of them looked like he was about to clock out, moaning and clutching his stomach. The other wounded man had blood pouring down his face.

Feeling a wound on both sides of his shoulder Fist figured he'd been hit by a bullet rather than shotgun pellets. It throbbed like hell.

"Hey Fist," came a voice from above, "you're

fucked, give us the money and drugs and we'll let you walk."

Fist knew who it was.

"That you Argo?"

"Yep, and you're trapped. Give us your gear and cash and we'll leave you to it."

"Ah go fuck yourself," Fist let out a pained chuckle.

"Pretty funny for a bloke who's wounded and has no way out. Give us the gear and money and you can go and get patched up."

Donkey, the only one of the four men not wounded, turned to Fist.

"Fist, tell him we haven't got any gear, and the money's out there in the bags."

"Shut the fuck up. We're not doing these pricks any favours," hissed Fist.

Donkey turned towards Argo and yelled, "the money's in the bags in the…" His sentence was cut short, as the butt of Fist's Glock smashed into his nose.

"Do that again, and I'll put a bullet through your head you weak prick." The business end of Fist's Glock rested against Donkey's temple. White specks of spittle had formed at the corners of Fist's mouth.

"Righto you two," Argo said to his driver and another of his men. "Get the car and do a quick drive-by and pick up those bags."

The two nominated men looked less than enthusiastic.

"We'll keep their heads down. The bags are miles away, there's no way they can hit you if you're quick."

The doubt was obvious on the men's faces.

"Just fuckin' get on with it, you weak fuckers," said Argo with menace, the barrel of his pistol moving in the general direction of the men.

The two men crawled backwards on to the road where they could stand, out of sight of Fist and his men. They walked back to get the car.

"What the fuck?" said Luny aloud, as the gun fire broke out on the other side of the clearing. He had the engine running and the car in gear, just about to attempt the escape up the steep incline. He ducked down half expecting bullets to come flying at him.

That's heaps more guns than before, Luny thought to himself. He dared a look up and across the clearing. He could see the bikies around the other side of their car shooting up towards the road. Followed their aim Luny saw four men lying near the road edge firing down at the Mongrels.

Luny snatched the radio.

"Dek, someone's shooting at the bikies, let's fuckin' go."

Luny, jammed his car into gear and dumped the clutch. He had only a couple of metres before he arrived at the base of the steep bank. The car crawled slowly forward in low range.

He aimed the car into the brush keeping it as square as possible to the hill to avoid rolling.

"Here we go," he said out loud. "Just keep it straight."

The Hilux crashed through the light scrub and saplings that bordered the camping area, the engine roaring in the low gear. The nose of the vehicle came up quickly, the wheels clawing for traction on the steep incline. The wheels spun in the dry dusty soil but kept the vehicle moving forwards and upwards.

"I can't see shit," Luny continued out loud, the steepness of the bank reducing his field of vision to blue sky and the tops of the tallest trees. He felt sure the ute must tip over backwards.

After what seemed an eternity to Luny, the front of the vehicle dropped suddenly as he reached the top, the ground flattening in front of him. He found himself heading across the gravel road. He swung the wheel sending the vehicle to the left and then jammed on his brakes looking to see whether Dek was following.

"Come on Dekky boy."

Dek waited until Luny was about half-way up and could wait no more. He followed directly behind and sent the vehicle up the steep incline. He could do nothing other than keep it straight and his foot to the floor, the engine howling in protest.

He almost collided with the back of Luny's ute when he topped the rise.

"Great work Dek," said Luny over the radio. "Knock it into high range four wheel drive and let's go."

The two utes headed off along the gravel road as fast as they could.

Both groups of bikies glanced to see the utes roaring up through the bush and back on to the road, but both groups had other priorities at that time.

Argo's men had brought their car up the road near the entry to the camp ground and stopped.

"I'll go in quick and stop beside the packs, you lean out and grab them. Be fuckin' quick."

"Make sure you stop with my side facing away from those fucking Mongrels," said his passenger.

That hadn't been the driver's plan. The driver

stomped on the accelerator sending the car down into the camping area and towards the two lonely backpacks. He stopped in a slide, yelling at his accomplice to do his job.

Shots rang out from the road as Argo and the other man poured shots into the vehicle below.

Fist stayed on the ground out of Argo's firing line but had a clear view of the car across the clearing. He took a bead on the driver and squeezed the trigger. It was a long shot.

The bullet missed by inches passing through the open driver's side window and out the passenger's open window causing no damage to the vehicle.

The driver heard the passage of the bullet as it passed through and yelled at his passenger to hurry.

"Got 'em, go."

The driver didn't need to be told twice, he stomped again on the accelerator generating a cloud of dust as the car slid around and fish tailed back out of the camping area, almost getting airborne as it crested the entry road.

Argo ran across the road and jumped into the car with the other bikies.

"Righto, let's fuck off," he yelled at the driver.

The car headed back towards Moruya.

"Give me the bags."

Argo grabbed the zipper and opened up the first bag.

"What the fuck," he yelled. "Stop the fuckin' car."

Opening the other bag he paused and then let out a loud guffaw. "Sneaky fuckers."

Fist heard the doors slam and the car head off. He pulled his phone from his pocket and made a call to Sydney.

Luny and Dek had reached Araluen before either spoke.

"Who the fuck was shooting from the road," said Luny into his radio.

"Might be best not to have this chat now."

"Sorry, you're right, let's just get home."

"Which way?" asked Dek as they drove through Araluen.

"Let's take the highway, I think it might be better to have some company."

They turned back onto the highway at Braidwood, giving way to a Harley as it headed down the main street towards the coast.

"That looked like a Mongrel," said Luny nervously.

"Let's just keep going," said Dek.

They drove in silence to the outskirts of Canberra.

"My place?" Dek asked into his handset.

"Yeah, let's get your car and return these utes."

They parked in Dek's driveway and walked into the house before either man spoke, both men flopping down onto Dek's white leather couch.

"What just happened? Who were those other guys?" asked Dek.

"Well, we're alive," said Luny. "I have no idea who the other guys were or why they were there. Let's just have a think," he said holding his hands to his head, "can anyone find us? I don't think so. No one really saw us. I reckon the only real link is the utes. They can't have been cops. Fuck I'm stuffed. What a fucking day. What a fucking day. All that and no money. Fuck. Let's get rid of those utes and get pissed."

Dek didn't offer any answers to Luny's questions or make any comments.

Walking back to the garage, "Let's get all the gear out, better not leave the guns behind," said Luny.

He was about to climb back into the ute when Dek finally spoke, "You might want to check behind the passenger seat."

"No, I've got everything."

"Not quite," said Dek.

Luny clicked the lever under the side of the passenger seat. The seat back tilted forwards.

"What the fuck…what is that…how did you…?

"I stuffed our overalls in the backpacks when I went to get them after I tipped the money out. We'd been through too much, I couldn't just give it back."

"What if the other group hadn't started shooting, and the Mongrels had found these. They would have killed us."

"Well, I didn't think we were going to be best friends with them no matter what happened, and I felt like we'd earned it."

"Man, I don't know whether to slap you or kiss you. Fuck, get a bag, let's get this stuff inside and get rid of these utes. I never want to see a Toyota Hilux again!"

Returning Luny's vehicle that was largely unscathed by the day's event wasn't a problem. However, Dek's ute had a broken rear window and a few pockmarks on the rear of the cab from shotgun pellets.

"Glad I took out the excess cover," said Dek. The woman on the counter of the rental company gave them a frosty greeting when she saw the rear window but said nothing, noting Dek's insurance option.

Sitting in Dek's Honda, Dek asked the question that neither had dared think about until this point.

"So, how much do you think is there?"

"I have no idea," chuckled Luny, " Let's get to your place and count it."

14

It was dark and cold when the three vehicles pulled into the campground near Araluen. Fist and his two surviving men had spent four very uncomfortable hours waiting after he had made the call to Sydney. One of the car occupants had called Fist from Moruya to make sure that Fist's group had not been discovered.

Fist's shoulder was throbbing, he struggled to find the focus to deal with all that had happened, and more importantly, to deal with what might be coming. He'd lost quite a bit of blood, and felt lightheaded. The severely wounded man had died, and Donkey was not looking good.

The men from Sydney loaded the dead man into the boot of the bullet-riddled hire car and winched the car onto a trailer, covering it with a tarpaulin. The car would disappear and be reported stolen, the dead man would just disappear. It was the ways things worked.

Unfortunately for the club, Fist had not taken out the excess insurance cover on the car. It was going to cost a bomb for this mistake.

Fist and the other two men were bundled into another vehicle and driven back to Sydney where a doctor with a love of cash work, would see what he could do for the two injured men. Fist was sure he would recover from his wound. It was his long-term future that concerned him more.

Luny and Dek sat in Dek's lounge staring at the shopping bag full of money. Dek broke the tension, giggling, and all but diving into the bag, throwing wads of notes towards Luny. Luny quickly got into the spirit of things, pegging a batch of hundreds at Dek's head.

The eventually sat back laughing.

"Doesn't look much," said Dek, sobering a little.

"Let's see."

Luny flicked through a couple of bundles, all fifty and hundred dollar denominations.

"Write down these numbers and then tally them," he said.

They worked for the next few minutes. Luny looked up at Dek.

"Well, how much."

"Seven-fifty," said Dek, in a flat tone, like he doubted what he had said.

"Holeeeeee shit," a big grin cracking Luny's face, "Seven hundred and fifty thousand buckeroos, holeeeeeee shit."

"Holeeeeee shit indeed," was all Dek could add.

"Got anything to drink?" suggested Luny.

The two men were enjoying a bottle of Dek's best Chardonnay—not Luny's first choice in drinks—when Dek thought to turn on the ABC Seven o'clock news.

The lead story was about the shooting of a young female Canberra police officer near a small town in southern NSW, and the death of a man, shot by NSW police, in another nearby Candelo. The man was suspected of being a motorcycle gang member. The police were working on potential links between the two events. Three members of a motorcycle gang, arrested in Bega, were assisting police with their enquiries. The young police woman had been airlifted to a Canberra hospital.

Luny and Dek stared at each other, mouths open.

15

Turd's second shot had creased the side of Rider's head. A few millimetres to the left and she would

have died instantly. Instead, the shot had knocked her unconscious. Like most head wounds it had been followed by copious amounts of blood, which had convinced Turd that she was dead.

Rider had woken a few minutes after Turd's departure. Her vision swam and she was unsteady on her feet but very much alive. The bullet to her shoulder had also clipped her, taking a chunk of flesh with it but leaving a superficial wound.

Staggering like an old drunk she made her way back towards the road, her head pounding with every step she took. The climb up the final embankment was torturous for her, forcing frequent stops for rest.

When she made it to the road, she all-but collapsed into the shade of big gum.

She had only been there a matter of minutes when she heard a car coming. Not until this point had she considered that the bikie might return. She felt very vulnerable on the edge and tried to rise, only making it to her knees before the car rounded the final corner. She pulled her gun from its holster and tried to raise it. The last thing she thought, before collapsing into unconsciousness into the gravel, was that the lights flashing in her eyes must have been something to do with her head injury.

The reality was, they were the flashers on top of a NSW Police vehicle. The next time she came to, was when the helicopter landed on the road. The paramedics staunched the bleeding to her wounds, mummifying her head in a swathe of white bandage. She was loaded on board and flown to Canberra.

"First Constable Octavia Rider." Rider said it out loud, rolling it around her tongue like she was sampling a nice red. There was no one else in her apartment. She laughed, "I like the sound of that."

Rider had received her promotion in an impromptu ceremony arranged in her hospital room with senior members from several police services present, along with her parents, and a couple of news reporters.

She had only spent four days in hospital and was now at home for a couple of weeks. Rider's career was on the trajectory she had planned. It was Plumber who had made the joke to her in private, that it was upwards with a bullet.

She was surprised that her mother seemed to want to make a fuss over her as well. Not only attending the ceremony but visiting regularly in the hospital and to her apartment where she was continuing her convalescence. She was more surprised that she enjoyed her mother's ministrations.

She had admitted to no-one that being shot in the head had been a small price to pay for the outcomes. What pleased Rider as much as the promotion itself was the fact that no-one in the history of the ACT Police had attained this rank in such a short period of time.

Rider realised that the fuss around her from her superiors was most likely due to the media coverage of an operation that had been a complete disaster, with the police services looking for some good news to come out of it. She could live with that.

One bikie was dead and a couple of others had

faced court on weapons-related charges but no drugs or money had been recovered.

It was obvious to Rider and the police services that something had gone wrong near the mountain, involving the mysterious white utes. The utes and the drivers had never been found. The bikies, of course, would say nothing about the operation.

The only smudge on the horizon for Rider, was Senior Detective Ross Plumber. When Rider was released from hospital Plumber was quick to continue the liaison that had started during the operation, becoming a frequent visitor to Rider's apartment during her recovery.

Rider initially enjoyed the attention and the potential benefits it might bring to her career. She was happy that Plumber was married as she had no intention for the relationship to continue indefinitely.

When she first met Plumber she had seen him as a strong and articulate senior officer who was well respected. Of course, he was like most of the males in the service, a bit rough and often inappropriate, particularly where women were concerned. But she was drawn to his policing intellect and standing within the service. It came as a complete surprise when she discovered that Plumber was very needy.

At first she enjoyed manipulating the situation,

getting him to run little errands for her, pouting when he denied her anything and rebuffing many of his frequent requests to have sex. It did not take long for Rider to have Plumber wrapped around her little finger. It took an equally short time for Rider to lose her respect for someone she saw as weak and vulnerable. She was more disappointed than anything else, having put Plumber on a pedestal only to find out he had the same vulnerabilities and insecurities as so many other people.

So what was initially an exciting and useful arrangement for Rider had started to become tiresome. Plumber's professions of love and suggestions that he might leave his wife did nothing to increase Rider's flagging interest, they served only to eat away at the little respect she might have still had for him.

While she made no attempt to end the relationship—she still saw value in it—she left Plumber in no doubt as to where her interests lay and her views on their future together. During her recovery at home, Rider had a lot of time on her hands. Her mind was far too active to be satisfied with daytime television, Internet shopping or DVDs. What occupied Rider's mind most were the two white utes involved in the operation that had nearly cost her life.

The utes were the key to what had gone wrong with the operation.

Rider had cajoled Plumber into bringing home the files relating to the case, something that could've landed him in hot water were it known. Rider was convinced she could find a clue that others had overlooked.

The three bikies who had been detained in Bega and charged with firearms offences provided no clue as to what had happened on the day. Not that this had surprised the police. Bikies with loose lips lived very short lives.

The only bikie that could be tied to the operation was Michael Ainslie—or Turd, as he was known in the club—but he was occupying an urn on someone's mantle.

No vehicles matching the two utes had been reported stolen in the region. It really had come to a dead end but Rider was not keen to let it go. A raid on the Mongrels' clubhouse found nothing but did allow the police the opportunity to recover their listening device. The officer who placed the device was a little perplexed when he discovered that his key would not open the padlock he had placed on the door leading under the house. It began to make more sense when he found a second bug.

Rider only became aware of this when se read the files. The device was traced to a company in China but that was a far as the investigation progressed down that particular path. The investigating officers were fast losing interest. Given no money or drugs had been recovered, the case was destined for the out-tray.

Rider was not keen to let it slide so easily.

Fist's house was raided as well. Fist's wife said she didn't know where the police might find her husband. She actually didn't know where he was, only that he was alive. She didn't explain this. The search didn't reveal anything.

Fist screwed up his nose as he took in his surroundings. He sat at the dining table of a house in Sydney's western suburbs, a white sling supporting his left arm. He had arrived there several days earlier in a semi-conscious state having lost a lot of blood.

The doctor had confirmed Fist's self-diagnosis that it was a bullet, and had passed through the fleshy part of his shoulder. Fist was very lucky. Thankfully, he knew his blood type, so the doctor was able to take blood from one of the other club members and give Fist a transfusion. For Fist this was another matter he'd deal with down the track, he would have a debt to pay.

Fist hadn't been told much by the senior club members who had come to talk to him, other than the cops were looking for him. When Fist had asked about his other injured man his question went unanswered.

The club hierarchy had decided that rather than explain a bullet wound, Fist would need to stay put until his shoulder was a bit better before he could go back to Canberra and face the inevitable questioning from the cops. And, Fist thought moodily, that would mean staying in this shit hole for way too long. But, at least he was still alive. Club members had disappeared for lesser transgressions than losing seven-hundred-and-fifty-thousand dollars.

Fist had asked repeatedly about reprisals against the Ferals. The more he asked the more he realised that the powers in Sydney were luke-warm on the idea, far more interested in getting the ice lab in Canberra running smoothly again.

A senior member had told Fist that the Ferals claimed they didn't have the cash, that it had been taken by the thieves in the white utes. While the lost cash was an issue it was not nearly as important as the money they were losing with the ice lab out of action. The young cook had weeks ago run out of pseudo-ephedrine, and rectifying this was the club's first priority.

This reaction just reinforced Fist's belief that the club, all clubs, had lost their way. No loyalty. Money, money, fuckin' money. Fuck this, thought Fist, I won't be letting this go.

16

It was almost lunchtime on a Saturday morning as the waiter slid two coffees onto the cool stainless steel of the table.

The taller man in the wrinkled t-shirt, seated with his back to the wall, tore the end from one of the two thin cylinders of sugar provided on his saucer, upending the entire contents into his flat white, casting the empty tube onto the table top. He stirred the coffee vigorously and took a quick sip, sighing with pleasure as the caffeine bit into his not-insubstantial hangover.

"Needed that, now's where's our eggs benny," he said, rubbing his hands together.

The smaller man watching from the other side of

the table said nothing but gave a small nod, a hit of a smile creasing his lips.

Luny couldn't believe the changes in Dek in only a few short weeks. Gone were the carefully pressed shirts, along with the hair product. It was obvious to Luny that the operation—which was what they called it—had been a tonic for Dek. His work seemed to bother him less. He actually laughed about the behaviour of his boss and then laughed even harder when he was offered the opportunity to deputise, in a long-term capacity, in the Branch Head position while the Shark was seconded to a taskforce. Things had fallen into place for Dek.

When Luny's phone rang he looked at the caller ID but did not answer it.

"Stella again?"

"Yep."

"Not answering?"

"I'll call her later."

Things had changed for Luny as well, perhaps not as drastically as they had for Dek, but there were changes nonetheless.

Things had certainly changed for Rider, especially when she returned to work. Her promotion, among her peers, was met with a mixture of jealousy and awe, which seemed to run about fifty fifty.

She was quite the celebrity sitting at her desk with her arm in a sling and a small adhesive patch above her right ear, largely covered by her hair. She had asked to come back to work earlier than necessary. Her boss agreed under the proviso that she would be desk-bound for several more weeks. This had been Rider's plan all along. She wanted access to some resources to continue her investigation.

Her first morning on the job saw a constant stream of senior and junior police coming past to wish her well and to hear the details of what had happened. She was even invited to a few social events. Even her boss, who had been more-than-a-little pissed off about her going over his head to Plumber to be part of the operation, had softened and welcomed Rider back, telling her to take it easy for a while.

Once the rush had died down, after her first day back, Rider began to go through the operation files again. She pondered the white utes, it was the only detail without closure. There'd been nothing stolen around the time. They wouldn't have been stupid enough to use their own cars, surely not.

She decided to head out for a morning coffee and stretch her legs. Sitting for long periods, for some reason, made her shoulder wound hurt. Her head wound gave her no issues at all. She stopped at the kerb waiting for the lights to change. Looking sideways, she saw two young men staring at her from the front seats of a car. One of them smiled. She smiled back as they drove away, the smile freezing when she saw the sticker on the rear window showing it was a hire vehicle. Surely not. It was an avenue to pursue at least.

She continued to the coffee shop, ordering her long black, long ago having given up milk and its fattening properties. She paid and rushed back to her desk, a little excited by the prospect of a lead to follow.

Her first stop was Google where she discovered there were a dozen or so hire hire firms in Canberra. The next thing to do would be to call them all and ask if they hired out Toyota Hilux utes and if so, were any hired out on the date of the operation. She thought it a logical direction to pursue, her only concern was whether she might get into trouble for pursuing it without good reason.

She called Plumber. He was happy to speak to Rider but not happy about what she wanted to do, telling her for the umpteenth time that the investigation had been concluded. The only outstanding task was a chat with Fist, if and when he turned up again in Canberra. But it didn't take long for her to cajole him into agreeing, a reminder that he was keen to visit her apartment that night, tipping the balance of the argument.

She started making calls.

Fist's shoulder was far from healed but he was prepared to forgo the sling in an effort to convince others that he was ready to return to Canberra.

He'd only been home a day when a knock on the door revealed Detective Plumber and an offsider.

"Mr Ellery, welcome home," said Plumber through the screen door, showing his badge. "Got time for a little chat." Before Fist had a chance to speak he added, "here or at the station, your choice."

"Always happy to oblige the Police," Fist responded, keeping his expression neutral. He had expected a visit, but not this soon, realising they must have been keeping an eye out for him. He had been interviewed many times over the years. He sometimes thought he could get a job at one of those fancy PR agencies or a law firm, teaching people how to deal with the cops.

"We just have a few questions about one of your members trying to kill a police officer down towards the coast, a month ago." Fist took the men into his kitchen where they sat at the table.

"I remember reading about that," said Fist. "An unfortunate business. But, I was glad to hear that the young lady pulled through okay."

"Hmmm, I'm sure you were. What was he doing there?"

"No idea, we don't monitor our members twenty four-seven."

"Three other members were arrested, not far from there, all carrying guns, know anything about that?"

"Nope."

"Where were you when it happened?"

"Me and some of the boys had a nice drive to Nowra for the day. Had lunch and then come home in the afternoon. I've even got a credit card receipt from the cafe if you'd like to see it."

"That all sounds very romantic," said Plumber, realising, not unexpectedly, that he wasn't going to get anything out of this discussion.

"And where have you been for the past couple of weeks?"

"Here and there. A bit of business, which is none of yours," Fist said looking straight into Plumber's eyes. "Now, if there's nothing further, I've got things to do." Fist started to rise, giving a small wince, as he pushed off the table to rise.

"In some pain Mr Ellery?"

"Just a bit of a muscle tear, nothing for you to concern yourself with," Fist added, deadpan, escorting the detectives to his front door.

"Thanks Mr Ellery, you've been very helpful. If I've forgotten anything I know where you live."

Fist said nothing further, shutting the door before the detectives had turned away.

He walked back to the kitchen and made himself a cuppa.

17

Rather than a comic store visit, or a Zildi wander, Luny and Dek spent the afternoon in Dek's garage, installing a safe.

After a bit of research Luny had decided that the centre of the floor was the best spot. But it was no small operation. They had to cut through the concrete slab and then dig a hole in the dirt underneath, cementing the safe into position and then covering it with a piece of carpet.

Not unlike the operation to place the listening device, Luny quickly realised that the bulk of the labor and thinking would fall on his shoulders.

He cut the required shape with a grinder into the concrete slab. Then had come the big job, punching through the concrete with a mini jackhammer. This had taken many hours of effort and no little sweat, from a man who was not used to manual labour.

Dek hovered like a worried mother, providing regular refreshments and moral support, doing his best to make himself useful. He was also prepared to take Luny's pointed jibes that grew throughout the afternoon.

It was early evening before Luny had the concrete removed to his satisfaction and the necessary amount of dirt removed from underneath. He threw down the hand trowel he had been using into the pile of dirt on the garage floor, sinking down beside the pile.

"I'm fucked. That'll do for today."

Dek had bought Wagyu steaks for dinner, and prepared them while Luny used the shower.

"So, how are we going to manage the money?" Luny asked, taking a sip from the Clare Valley shiraz that Dek had bought for him.

"What do you mean?"

"Well, how much cash can we spend at once, how much do we carry. I still get a bit nervous about someone noticing our increased cash habits. We'll have to be careful. Should we split it into two piles and spend our own. Or do we keep it together, and have an allowance each week?"

"I hadn't really thought about it," said Dek. "I figured we'd just spend it when we wanted to."

"Great, but what happens if one of us wants to buy something big. And what's the upper limit we should have for using cash, you know, the suspicion-free threshold?"

"This is far more stressful than I thought it would be," frowned Dek, his glass of Cloudy Bay savignon blanc, half way to his lips.

"I warned you, the laundering is where people get caught, we can't afford to get slack with our habits. I think we'll have to divide the money into two portions and draw from our own stash, consulting if we wan't to buy something that might be pushing the boundaries. This steak is fucking fantastic, by the way," Luny said, another fork-full about to dock with the mothership.

After dinner they divided the money into two piles.

I'll go out tomorrow morning while you're working and buy a couple of sturdy bags in two different colours to keep it in."

"Yeah, and I'll keep sweating my balls off in your garage."

Dek ignored the comment.

"What about a trip to Europe some time?" he asked, "a bit of reward for our efforts."

"Yeah, I had been thinking of something like that. We could pay for most of it using cash, and certainly the spending money."

"I'll start doing some research," said Dek, excitement obvious in his tone.

Rider had mixed success with her phone calls. Two of the rental agencies refused to provide any information until she visited in person to prove that she was, indeed, a police officer. Several others didn't rent Hilux utes.

In the end she was left with two firms to visit, and from a third agency, the details of a person who had rented out a Hilux ute during the date in question.

Rider was a little nervous about her next step. Her boss still wasn't aware that she was continuing to investigate the failed operation. She knew she could rely on Plumber's support if required, but even if Plumber smoothed it over, she was concerned about putting her boss offside, particularly with her new-found reputation. She didn't want to tarnish it already. In the end she decided to drive out to the agencies in her own vehicle but in uniform. She would merely leave work a little earlier, which wouldn't be an issue with her current flexible work arrangements.

She decided she would see what the visits revealed before she actually called anyone. And given the only information she had related to a single ute she wondered whether she would bother at all.

The first hire company was a quick visit. She got a little annoyed when she was advised that they didn't even have Hilux utes. When she asked why they hadn't told her that on the phone, the young guy on the counter just shrugged and said it wasn't him who had spoken to her.

The last place was a little more rewarding.

The young woman on the counter, once it was established that Rider was a cop, was happy to hand over details of another ute that had been hired out over the period of the operation.

"I actually remember this one. The ute came back with some damage, a broken rear window and a few other scratches."

Rider returned to her car, feeling a little flat, having hoped that she would find two utes hired from one place. It took her back to square one. She sat tapping her fingers on the steering wheel.

That night, as Plumber lay dozing in post-coital slumber beside her, Rider ran the information through her head again. She felt she had been on to something.

She prodded Plumber in the ribs to wake him. She was very keen that he didn't stay the night. She wanted to give Plumber's wife no excuses for kicking him out. She had started to wonder if Plumber was angling towards that outcome.

As Plumber put his clothes on she ran her findings past him—she would have done it when he arrived but given his enthusiasm for her it was hard to get him to concentrate on anything until after he had achieved the evening's goal.

"What if they hired them from different places. Maybe they were smart enough not to leave an obvious trail."

"I thought of that, it just seems unlikely."

"Did you check the hire dates, do they coincide?"

"Shit," Rider slapped her own forehead, "I never thought of that."

"That's why I'm a detective and you still wear a uniform, very nicely I might add."

Rider didn't rise to either point, she was already thinking about getting the information from the hire companies. She had a good feeling about it.

The next morning she was in the office early, calling the two hire companies as soon as they were open for business.

By the end of the second phone call her heart rate had risen, the hire dates matched.

Fist was a different man since the psuedo buy had gone wrong. It was obvious to Sandra, his wife. It had showed the minute he had arrived home.

She had been excited to see him. Their child was due in less than three weeks, and she had felt vulnerable and lonely with him away, but as a long-time club wife she understood how things worked. But now the excitement was mounting for her again. It was their first child, and would be their only one. They had long given up on the idea of children. Sandra had fallen pregnant on two occasions after many years of trying, losing both babies within eight weeks. When it happened this time, Sandra was forty.

She had smiled many times about her husband's poor efforts to conceal the excitement of a son or daughter. It wasn't a bikie thing to show too much excitement about anything, least of all things on the home front, like kids.

Compared to most men in the club, she knew that Fist treated her far better than other members treated their wives and partners. Even though she knew that Fist subscribed to the view that it was colours first and everything else second, he went out of his way to minimise the impact of this on their lives.

But he had changed in the time he was away. She didn't know much about what had happened. It had always been their agreement that he only gave her scant details of anything the bikies were up to. This way she couldn't be implicated in anything that might have happened. She knew that there had been a problem with stolen money and that a couple of the blokes had disappeared from the Canberra club. And of course, she knew her husband had been shot.

The only thing she understood for certain was her husband's hatred of the Ferals and particularly, Argo, their leader in Canberra. Fist had never liked the Ferals, they were rivals, but his dislike had escalated way beyond this on his return. It was the only thing Fist had spoken to her about. She knew Fist wanted to hurt Argo and had been warned off by Sydney. But she knew her husband. He would not let it go. And this worried her.

Rider sat at her desk, trying to suppress the excitement she felt, now that she had the information she needed. Surely it was too much of a coincidence that the hire dates for the two vehicles matched, particularly as it wasn't over a weekend. The thing that troubled her was what to do next.

If she mentioned it to her boss, Senior Sergeant Bob Nolan, she would likely get a lecture and be told to leave it alone and get back to her own work. She knew she had already pushed the envelope with him by going directly to Plumber to arrange for her to participate in the drug operation. Nolan had softened his stance in light of Rider's injuries and promotion with things largely back onto an even keel. Rider was a little nervous about messing with this.

She was also worried about taking the information to Plumber. He had largely tolerated her ongoing interest in pursuing the case, treating her like a favoured child, all-but patting her on the head. The reason, of course, was that he only ever had one thing on his mind. But rather than be annoyed by Plumber's treatment of her, Rider continued to use it to get what she needed.

But Rider knew Plumber well enough, that even with his obsession with her, if he saw that she had a fresh lead, he wouldn't hesitate to grab her information and act on it.

Rider chewed on her thumb nail, staring into the distance.

She smacked her palms down on the desk, coming

to a decision. She would just take things a little further on her own. She would be doing Plumber a favour, finding out whether she got a sense from either of the men that they might have been involved. It would save wasting the time of senior detectives. If she got a sense of something awry she would definitely pass the information on but if it looked like a simple coincidence then she would not be wasting Plumber's time and manpower.

A very sensible approach she thought to herself.

Rather than call them, she decided to wait until after work when she could approach the men at home.

It was her first full day back at work. Her wounds were healing nicely. Her shoulder was still a bit sore but she was largely back to full health. She had even started some light training in the gym, doing some walking on a treadmill that had evolved into a slow jog.

And being back at work she had been assigned a marked car to drive home for the week. She thought this and the uniform would send a strong message to both of the men, perhaps eliciting the kind of reaction she hoped to see.

She stayed a little late at work to give the men time to get home. At five thirty she climbed into the police car and headed the short distance to the closer of the two addresses. She enjoyed driving the marked cars and the impact this had on the traffic around her. It was a power rush. When they saw her, other drivers became painfully scrupulous in obeying the traffic rules, ironically, almost to a point of causing accidents. She tried not to smile when she saw the fear in some faces when she happened alongside.

On this day she drove up behind a Subaru wagon and could see the driver using his mobile phone as he sat waiting for the traffic light to change. She honked her horn. The man looked in the mirror with the beginnings of a look of annoyance, until he realised it was a cop car. He dropped the phone into his lap like it had burned his hand.

She didn't want to be bothered by a driver stop, when she had something so important to do, so instead of pulling the driver over, she stomped on the accelerator, giving him the evil eye as she slowed, level with him. She pulled back in behind the car and followed him along until she needed to turn off to the left, leaving the man in no doubt that he was very lucky.

She put the annoying driver out of her mind, focusing, instead, on the first address and the first name: Deklin Stephens. What sort of name is Deklin, she wondered. She smiled, no worse than Octavia.

Dek plonked onto his couch, a glass of white to hand on the coffee table. He took a sip, letting the crisp, dry, fruity New Zealand sauvignon blanc spill over his tongue. Dek had always seen himself as a bit of a white wine snob, favouring some very pedestrian Chardonnays, and willing to bend someone's ear about it, as he did with his coffee obsession. But now that he could afford the better drops, he talked less about it and just enjoyed the product.

Life had taken a positive turn for him in a short time. With the cash sitting safely underneath his car and the garage floor Dek felt a sense of well-being that he hadn't experienced since he was a kid.

And he knew it was as much about how they got the cash, as actually having it. The thrill he had felt when they stopped the bikies on the mountain road would come back to visit whenever he thought about what had happened, coursing through his body like a shot of adrenalin. He had never felt such power, nor felt so alive and in control. He had wanted to jump out of his skin at the time. He remembered the pent-up energy that had surged through him. The fear he had felt when the bikies had them cornered was nothing compared to the euphoria he still felt about getting out of there. It had been a great day in his life.

And his confidence had grown in leaps and bounds as a consequence. He liked himself a lot more than he had in a long time. The irony, as he saw it, was that now that he had more money for finer things, he wanted them less. And this made him happy as well, realising that his previous focus on material things had been largely driven by a lack of self-respect and maybe even a bit of self-loathing.

That was not to say, he smirked to himself, that he didn't enjoy spending the money. He was super excited about the Europe trip with Luny. Dek was chuffed that Luny was happy to go with him. Dek realised that Luny could have done something with Stella instead, but had not hesitated in agreeing to go with him. The plans were well advanced, including how best they could maximise spending cash from the safe, instead of using credit cards.

They had agreed that paying for the business class flights in cash was an acceptable risk and they would both take ten thousand dollars in cash with them, the maximum amount they could take out of the country without having to declare it.

Yes, things were going well for Dek as he saw it. He had his promotion at work. He had even thought about what they might do once the cash started running low. He hadn't broached it with Luny, there was plenty of time for that.

Life was good.

And then the doorbell rang.

Luny was in a similar posture to Dek. He was working at a new level of some game or other and enjoying a glass of Margaret River red. Like Dek, Luny was also feeling a level of satisfaction with the way things had turned out.

Unlike Dek he didn't think about the happenings of the day in such a positive light. When he thought about it, the shivers up his spine were less about adrenalin and more about the fear of what might have happened. He realised they had got away by the skin of their teeth and but for an extreme measure of good luck they could both be dead. It was not a feeling he enjoyed.

Dek seemed to think that Luny was, like him, enjoying an increase in self-confidence, particularly in his relationship with Stella. Luny hadn't bothered to explain that he was wrong. It wasn't self-assurance or confidence that had given him a bigger say in things, it was the result of staring at his own mortality and realising that shit didn't matter. Perhaps, Luny thought, the end result was the same as Dek felt, but he didn't think so. If anything, he felt far more introspective, questioning things far more than he had since uni.

But, all that aside, he smirked, he did enjoy that feeling of well-being with the cash tucked away in the safe in Dek's garage.

And then his mobile rang, it was Dek.

"Hey."

"Don't fucking speak, just listen. A cop just came to visit me at home. She asked about hiring the ute, what I wanted it for, how long I had, where I went. She asked if I knew you, I said no. I didn't know what else to say."

Luny sat up straight on the couch.

"You're shitting me?"

"No, fuck, I wouldn't lie about this sort of thing. She's probably on her way to visit you. You need to get your story straight. I don't think I was very convincing. I was shaking. I told her that I had to move some furniture, nothing much more. She seemed to accept it, but it's hard to tell. Just don't tell her you know me."

Luny walked over to his window which looked out over the car park and street. Before he had a chance to speak a police car pulled up and a young police woman stepped out.

"She's here, I can see her on the road below. I'll call you back." Luny broke the connection without waiting for a response from Dek.

He was shaking as well. He sat down, thinking he had to pull himself to together.

Quick, what can they know, he thought. They didn't arrest Dek so they can't know much. In fact, what have we done. Nothing, unless the bikies reported the robbery, which was never going to happen.

He calmed a little. A story, right. Can't say furniture, will look stupid. He was thinking this when there was a knock at his door.

Even in his state of fear he noticed that the policewoman was very attractive.

"Craig Lune?"

"Yes?" was all Luny said.

"My name is First Constable Octavia Rider, I wonder if you wouldn't mind me asking you a few questions about a vehicle you hired a few weeks ago."

This was same approach Rider had taken with Dek.

"Sure, come in," Luny tried to be calm and normal.

"You hired a Toyota Hilux ute for three days," said

Rider citing the exact dates. "Can I ask what you used the vehicle for and where you went."

"Sure, I rented it to take some rubbish away from my mother's house." He regretted saying it, as soon as it was out. What if she spoke to his mother? "I just did a few runs to the recycling centre and to a green waste depot."

"You didn't leave town?"

"No, can I ask what this is about?"

"It's just routine at this stage," said Rider wheeling out the line that they had learned in training.

"The rental agency said that the vehicle had some damage when you returned it, what happened."

"Oh, oh... I broke the rear window in the cab when I was loading some branches on."

Rider watched his eyes closely as Luny spoke. Luny held her gaze for the whole time. She scribbled in her note book.

"Do you know a man by the name of Deklin Stephens?"

"No, no, can't say I do."

Rider paused, closing her notebook and putting it back in her pocket.

"Thanks for your time Mr Lune, that's all I have at this time."

"Can you tell me what this is about?"

"As I said," Rider looked directly at Luny again, "it's just routine at this stage. I'll see myself out."

Luny followed her to the door, closing it after she had departed. He went back to the window to watch her get back into her car and drive away. He flopped onto the couch.

"Fuck," he said aloud.

He picked up his phone to call Dek. He paused, wondering if he should use a pay phone.

"Fuck, you're being an idiot," he said aloud and pushed Dek's number. Dek answered on the first part of the first ring.

"What happened?" Dek blurted.

"Same as you no doubt, she just asked what I had used the ute for and where I went, and whether I knew you. Look, I don't think we should worry too much. If they had something more they would have done something more. She was only a constable. If it was serious they would have sent detectives."

"I'm really scared," was all Dek said. "All I could think about before you rang, was Goulburn Super Max prison."

Luny snorted with laughter, releasing a bit of the tension he felt.

"It's not funny, maybe we should get rid of the money."

"Dek, listen to me. Calm down and think about it. We haven't even committed a crime, unless the bikies have reported it. And you and I both know that hasn't happened. They'll just be following up on some leads from that whole operation. They don't know anything. It's just a hiccup." Luny paused. "Dek, promise me, you won't do anything stupid with the money. Don't make me come over and change the combination."

"Okay, I won't do anything. And you're probably right. But I don't feel well."

"Be positive. We were smart renting the utes separately, and we haven't done anything stupid with money." Luny was selling a calm demeanour that he didn't necessarily feel but he knew, for both their sakes, he had to bring Dek back from the edge.

"You okay now, do I need to come over."

"No, no, don't come over. What if she came back. No, I'll be fine. Just stay there. I'll be fine.

"Okay, I'll go now. Just promise you'll call if you get wound again."

"Yep, I'll call, see you."

Luny sat back into his old couch to run through what had happened.

Fist smacked the bottle of Jack Daniels down onto the kitchen table with a force that woke his wife.

"What was that?" she said from the bedroom.

"Nothing, don't worry about it, go back to sleep."

Fist was not in a good way. He had drunk half a bottle of JD but felt completely sober. I should be happy he thought. I'm still alive and about to become a father.

But he could not move beyond the betrayal he felt from the club. He had given his life to them, and his reward for unquestionable, unswerving, loyalty was a kick in the balls, as he had put it to his wife.

He couldn't decide that the lack of action against Argo and the Ferals was punishment for him having lost the money or whether the club was more focused on getting the ice lab running at full capacity again. He had even lost control of that, Sydney telling him he needed to get better first.

Fuck that, he thought, and fuck the club. I'll do this on my own. He spent the next couple of hours mulling out a plan and finishing the remainder of the bottle.

He woke early, draped over the table. He winced and groaned as he moved his wounded shoulder. He made a cup of tea and thought about the plans he had made the night before. He decided he had to go ahead, he couldn't live with himself if he didn't right the wrongs.

His biggest concern was his wife and what he was going to tell her.

When he heard her ugg boots dragging up the hallway he steeled himself for the conversation.

"I want you to pack, you're going to Perth."

Still half asleep, his wife shook her head as if not hearing him clearly.

"What, what do you mean."

"I need you to pack and go to your sister's. There's some stuff going down and you and the baby may not be safe here." He had deliberately referenced the baby to lend weight to his argument.

"What do you mean, I'm due in a week, I'm set up for hospital here. I can't just go. And anyway," she added with certainty, "they won't let me fly at thirty eight weeks."

Fist winced, annoyed that he hadn't thought of that, knowing that she was right.

"Well, you'll have to go to your brothers or your mothers. I'll drive you."

"And what about hospitals and doctors, and my mid-wife, what do I fucking do about that?" she said on the verge of tears. "Fist you can't do this to me."

"Sit down," he said, his tone softening. "You have

to go. I know it's not ideal, but it won't be safe, I need you out of here. There's things happening and if you're around it will only take my focus away and it won't be good for either of us."

"And what about you?" she asked. "Are you coming back to me? Fucking great, a single mum before the baby's born."

"Look, you know the deal, I can't tell you anything, but it will go better for both of us, and the baby, if you're not here." He knew this was the best approach. "Just call your doctor and the hospital. They'll send your details. They'll have a good set up in Newcastle."

His wife was now crying. She didn't often cry.

"This is fucking great. I fucking hate you."

"Get your stuff together, we need to do this right away. You can make all the arrangements from Newcastle."

The four-and-a-half hour drive went very quietly. His wife said nothing to him. The only thing she had said, was to her mother, calling her and saying that she was coming to stay.

Fist carried his wife suitcases to the door to be met by the scowling face of his mother-in-law. Fist was used to that. Fist's wife disappeared inside the house without a farewell. Fist drove straight back to Canberra. He had to do this, he told himself again.

Rider didn't know what to do. She was sitting back at her desk the next day, mulling over the events of the previous evening, chewing on her thumbnail.

When she talked to Stephens, the way he reacted convinced her that she might be on to something. But after visiting the second guy, Craig Lune, she was nowhere near as sure.

It would be easy to put down Stephens' nerves to the fear that most people felt when they were dealing with cops, she thought. And given the second guy was so relaxed and his story so logical it seemed that the coinciding hire dates were just that, a big coincidence.

Short of following them how could she take this forward, she wondered, how could she work out if they had both done the same thing.

And then it came to her. The mileage. She slapped her forehead with the palm of her hand. Surely the hire companies kept a record of the mileage.

As it turned out, they did keep records. She learned two things that made her very excited. Firstly, the mileage on both vehicles was almost identical, and secondly, Rider decided, the distances were way beyond a few trips around Canberra, dropping off furniture or rubbish.

She pulled up a map on her computer and worked out that the mileage was easily far enough to cover the distance to where she had been shot and back again. In fact, the mileage was substantially more than that.

Rider still didn't think this was enough evidence to confront Plumber with, but she decided she would do a bit of weekend sleuthing. The missing piece of the puzzle was whether the two men knew each other.

And it didn't take very long to prove that they did.

Fist recognised that he was a bit obsessed with his plan to kill Argo, but not so obsessed that he didn't care if he himself was caught or killed. He wanted to get back to his wife and baby in one piece but with his mind at ease. It was simply a matter of honour that had to be upheld.

The only thing that really troubled him was that it would likely be the last thing he would do in his club colours. The only weapon he had was an old single-shot, sawn-off, he'd had for years. It wasn't ideal. He would need to be very close, but it would have to do. All the handguns, including his Glock, had disappeared after the shootout in the bush.

He knew where Argo worked and figured the early Saturday morning streets of an industrial area would be as good as spot as any to take him out. Most other options usually meant Argo having his men about him, and Fist didn't want another shoot out especially when he only had a single-shot weapon and no men with him. No, he thought, this is about me and Argo, has to be one-on-one.

He put a set of stolen rego plates, that he'd had stashed for years, on his wife's Toyota just in case anyone saw the car or if he was caught on a security camera.

He felt calm, almost peaceful, as he drove in the light traffic, the sun barely up. As he'd hoped, the industrial area was very quiet. He'd already driven the streets, the previous day, and had selected the spot he would park and wait for Argo. There was only one route he could take.

Fist parked and left the engine running. He hummed along to a tune on radio, the loaded shotty sitting in his lap.

A few cars had driven into the area while Fist was waiting. If Argo came by car, it would be much more difficult, Fist knew, he'd have to get him when he was getting out. It would make it a lot more complicated and increase the risk of getting caught or being seen.

A few more minutes had ticked by when Fist heard the approach of a Harley a couple of streets away.

When Argo's Harley turned the corner Fist accelerated hard, driving up quickly behind him, hoping Argo wouldn't see the car until the last second. Fist got close and leaned out the window. The good thing about the sawn-off, he knew, was that he didn't need to aim carefully, from that distance he wasn't likely to miss. He knew the shot was unlikely to kill him, but that was okay, he just wanted to bring him down, and then have the opportunity to look into his eyes before he fired another shot.

Fist pulled the trigger, the gun bucking in his outstretched hand. Argo went down hard in the middle of the road, the big bike skidding into the gutter and then bouncing back into the road after hitting the kerb.

Fist slammed on the brakes, reloading the gun as he stepped out through the door. Argo was writhing on the ground. He'd rolled onto his side, forced by the pain of the pellets embedded in his back. He could see Fist walking towards him and tried to stand, getting as far as his knees before Fist stood in front of him.

"G'day old son," said Fist.

"I haven't got your money," Argo blurted, wincing in pain. "We didn't get it."

"I don't give a fuck about the money Argo, there's a matter of principle here."

"I can get more."

"Have some self-respect Argo."

"Fuck you, you prick."

"That's more like it." Fist raised the gun and shot Argo in the face, the distance was very short.

Fist walked back to the car, not hurrying, got back in and drove away. It was another ten minutes before anyone happened across the gruesome scene in the middle of the street.

18

It was Saturday and Dek wondered whether they should still have breakfast together, given the visit from the policewoman had only occurred a couple of days before.

Luny thought Dek was being a bit too careful, understandable in the circumstances, but too careful nonetheless. Had Luny realised that Rider was following him in her car, he might have given Dek's concerns a little more attention.

Rider had parked her white Subaru a couple of bays over from Luny in the big underground garage. She had found it very easy to tail Lune in his old, beaten up Falcon. It was very easy to recognise in the traffic ahead of her. She climbed quickly out of her car and followed him at a discreet distance, experiencing a buzz from tailing her mark, as she called him in her head. She wasn't overly worried about Lune spotting her. Out of her uniform with a baseball cap on her head she doubted he'd recognise her.

Up a couple of escalators they both went, and across a busy city street. She stopped as she saw him enter the outside seating area of a busy sidewalk cafe, and sit down at a table with Deklin Stephens. She smiled to herself.

Before she had a chance to even think about what to do next, her phone rang, it was the young woman from the car hire firm which had rented one of the utes.

Fist drove home feeling like he'd had a spiritual awakening. His senses were clear and he felt a great weight lifted from his shoulders. It wasn't as if he enjoyed murder, but he knew that his life would not have been able to go on without cleaning the slate.

It had been simple and now he could go and be with his wife.

There would likely be repercussions, a distinct possibility that the club would cut him loose and maybe punish him before that. It was even possible that the cops would nab him if there had been a witness lurking somewhere. But he would worry about these issues if and when they arose, for now he felt like he'd just had his first snort of coke.

He laughed out loud, thinking if he could get the money back, then his slate would be truly clean. He spent the drive home thinking about the cluster fuck in the bush and getting shot by Argo. And then he had an epiphany.

He remembered it vividly, as if the wasting of Argo had opened up a blockage in a synapse. When he had leant out the window with the shotgun to shoot at one of the utes, a moment before its back window had exploded into a thousand shards he remembered what he had seen: a hire-car sticker.

"Fuck me," he yelled aloud. "Surely not."

He stopped and checked his phone for the nearest outlet. He drove there and found that they were not yet open. He went and bought a coffee from a nearby cafe and then a cap and the biggest pair of sunglasses he could find from a nearby work-wear shop.

As soon as the shop-front opened he walked in the door. The young woman, the only staff member at that time of the day, smiled and asked if she could help. Fist decided to start with the soft approach.

"Yeah, a car drove into mine and drove off a couple of weeks back and did a bit of damage. I didn't get the number but then I just remembered today that it had one of your stickers on the back window. I was hoping you could give me the details of who was driving it so I could contact them."

"I'm sorry to hear that sir, but unfortunately I can't pass on personal details, it's against company policy, and probably against the law."

Fist was pretty sure it would go this way, that's why he had bought the hat and glasses. His voice was slow and measured, but the menacing tone unmistakable.

"Ok, enough fucking around, I'm going to give you about thirty seconds to give me a name and address or I'll lock the front door and we'll talk about this a little more.

The young woman went pale.

"Ok, ok, please don't hurt me."

He gave her the make of vehicle and the date. The young woman gave a small start.

Fist sensed her surprise.

"What?" he demanded.

"It's, it's just that the police were asking about this same vehicle recently."

The young woman wrote Luny's name, address and telephone number on a yellow sticky note and handed it to Fist.

Fist thanked the young woman and apologised for scaring her. He climbed back into his car and drove home pondering what he had just learned. The cops were onto the fuckers as well.

And while Fist was pondering his next move, the young woman from the rental firm was dialling the number on the card that Rider had left behind.

"Hi, Constable Rider, it's Nadine from Carz. You were in the other day asking about the Hilux ute."

Rider could hear that the young woman's voice was shaky.

"Yes?" said Rider.

"I just had some bloke in here, he threatened me, and made me give him the same details you were after the other day. I was really frightened, I am really frightened, what should I do?"

"What did he look like?"

"He had tattoos up his arms and a ponytail. I couldn't tell much else, he had a cap on, and sunglasses."

"Okay. Look, I'm sure that's all he'll want, so he won't be coming back. Stay put and someone will come and talk to you."

"Okay. Should I call anyone else."

"No, leave it with me for now and I'll sort it out."

"Okay, thanks."

Rider broke the connection. This was starting to get serious. She knew she should call it in. But she didn't. She analysed what she had. She convinced herself that she still didn't have much. There was no evidence that the two in the cafe had broken the law. She couldn't arrest them for anything, all she could do was talk to them and try and get more information about what had happened. The only danger she saw was that it was likely that bikies were now on their case.

And far from being a problem, she thought, this could prove to be the leverage I need.

She tried to calm her breathing as she walked towards the cafe. She decided on a direct approach, grabbing a chair from an empty table and sitting down with the two men.

She realised that neither of them recognised her at first.

It was Dek who spoke first.

"Can we help you?" he asked in a forthright tone.

Rider pulled off her cap and sunnies.

Luny was first to twig, sitting back in his chair as if trying to will himself away from the woman. Dek wasn't far behind. His forthright manner withered, fear clutched at his insides.

Rider sensed that she had made the right entrance, and pounced on the opportunity she had created.

"Gentlemen, let's not mess about. You lied to me about not knowing each other. But worse than that, you're in some serious danger. I just had a call from a certain rental-car agency, that a bikie had just been in and coerced some details from the, very frightened, young lady who works there. Time is not on your side. I think you need my help."

Luny turned urgently towards Dek, thinking he would see a man on the verge of tears, needing to stop him blurting out things in a state of panic. He couldn't let him incriminate the both of them.

Luny need not have worried. What he saw shocked him, as it had when they had the bikies bailed up on the mountain road. Dek was almost smiling. The corner of his mouth had just the slightest upward turn. Luny watched as Dek, without rushing, removed his sun glasses, placing them carefully on the table next to his coffee cup. He looked directly into the eyes of Rider.

He spoke without haste.

"Listen, it doesn't fucking matter whether or not we know each other. We might have just met. And as to bikies being after us, I've no idea what you're talking about. You're interrupting our breakfast, if you've nothing to add, you might consider pissing off."

It was difficult to discern who was more taken aback, Rider or Luny. Rider spoke first.

"Look, I checked the mileage on your utes, they were almost identical and way beyond what you'd do for a few trips across Canberra. I know you were in the mountains with the bikies. Something happened and you two are involved. If it were me, and I knew that I had the Mongrels looking for me, I'd be looking for a friend who might be able to help you stay alive.

Luny started to respond but Dek raised his hand to forestall Luny's comment.

"Thanks officer, Rider was it? Thanks for the sage advice. We know where to find you, now, if you don't mind…"

Rider wasn't sure what to do next. Stephens was the one who had seemed the most nervous of the two when she had talked to them originally. She figured he would be the one to buckle first.

"Alright, have it your way. Here's my card. Give me a call if you change your mind."

Both men watched as Rider rose from the table walked away down the street.

Fist changed into his Mongrels gear and got back onto his Harley, his sawn-off secured inside the leather bucket strapped near his front forks. It was readily accessible but out of sight to the casual observer. He rarely carried it on his bike these days, if he needed a weapon, it was much easier to conceal a handgun but unfortunately he didn't have access to one.

He was happy to be back on his bike and in his club colours. He realised it was possibly his last run in them. He had already ignored a couple of phone calls from Sydney, figuring the word was already out about that rat-bastard, Argo.

He was still feeling the euphoria from his morning's work. However, it wasn't so strong to make him ignore warning signs that the cops were on to the two pricks in the white utes. He could just ignore them and head off to see his wife and only have the club to worry about. He wondered what it was that made him ignore the warnings.

He'd called his wife earlier. She still wasn't happy with him, but had at least talked to him. Nothing had changed in relation to the baby's arrival. She had sorted out the birthing arrangements with the local hospital and was a little more comfortable with things. Fist was confident he could patch things up.

He figured that if he was going to get the boot from the club he might as well see if he could scare the ute driver, whose details he had, into coughing up some of the cash they had taken. At least then he'd have a nest egg for his family. And if he survived the club's retribution the money would be enough to get something going.

The big Harley purred into life as he cranked the starter. He smiled, thinking he would never grow tired of the feeling of the eighty eight cubes throbbing between his legs. He pulled out onto the street and opened up the throttle, way beyond the speed limit in a few seconds, flipping the bird to a disgruntled looking woman, watering her garden bed, further up the street. He laughed out loud. It felt good to be doing something.

He parked on the street near the address that the women at the car rental agency had given to him. He slipped the sawn-off out of the boot and held it inside his jacket as he entered the building. The flat number was on the top floor. He was puffing slightly when he climbed the final flight of stairs and pounded on the door. No one answered. This was the only flat on the top floor, so he put the gun on the ground without fear of anyone seeing it, and pulled out his phone. There were a couple more missed calls from Sydney.

He punched in the mobile number the scared young woman had given to him.

"Fuck," said Luny, first to speak after Rider's departure, "fuck, we're fucked."

"Luny, stay calm."

Even in the panic he felt, Luny was still gobsmacked at Dek's altered persona and said as much.

"I don't get you. It's like what I saw on the mountain with the bikies. You change. Someone wants to kill you, and instead of pissing your pants, as I would've predicted you'd do, you go all calm and cool."

"Luny, Luny, Luny. Let's take a breath." Dek had slid down into his chair. "What has she got? She had nothing, otherwise she would've done something. She's got a bit of anecdotal evidence but she can't prove shit. And even if she could prove we were there, what was it that we did? Nothing, we've done nothing other than fibbing about knowing each other, they won't lock us up for that."

"That's fine, but what about the bikie getting a name? That's less good."

"Look, we don't even know if that's true, she's probably trying to bluff us. Let's not panic and do anything rash."

Before Luny could say anything further, his phone

rang. He looked at the screen, not recognising the number.

"Hello?" Luny didn't say any more than this for the next minute or say. But the changing pallor of his face, from white to ashen-grey, gave Dek some indication that all was not as it might be in Luny's world.

"I don't know what you mean. I only rented the ute to move some furniture. I never drove out of Canberra... I'm sorry if you don't believe me. You can't just ring me up like this and accuse me of something. How did you get my number? No, fuck you, I'm calling the cops."

Luny broke the connection.

"I'm dead, we're dead. That was a fucking bikie. He said he was calling from outside the door of my flat, telling me we owe him seven-hundred-and-fifty-thousand dollars. I repeat I'm dead." Luny's voice had gone up as his hysteria built.

"Shhhh, keep it down," said Dek, seeing that a couple of other diners had turned in their direction. "The bikies will know even less than the cops. Think about it. All they have is some details that you rented a ute at about the right time. He's got no idea if it was you on the mountain. You're response was good."

"Yeah, let's see how good my response is, if they are holding a blow-torch to my balls."

"Look," said Dek, "we need to think this through. Let's go down to Merimbula for the night, get out of town. You can stay a few days if we need to let things cool a bit."

"Yeah, that's a good idea. Do you reckon I can get some stuff from home?"

"Let's just drive past in my car. We'll be able to see if anyone's about and just keep going if they are."

"I'm not sure I can cope with this other side of you. What the fuck?"

"Look, let's not question it, let's just get on with it."

Fist swore when the phone connection was broken. He wasn't a hundred percent convinced the bloke he had been talking to was the bloke he was after, but there was still enough doubt there to explore it a little more. The guy was certainly nervous, but probably no more nervous than the average bloke when talking to an angry Mongrel.

He wanted a look at the guy. He had seen his face briefly when he had pulled along-side on the bush road near Moruya. He wasn't sure if he'd remember him but it was worth a look.

He walked down the stairs of the apartment block

and sat on his Harley wondering what to do next. His phone rang, it was Sydney again. He answered it.

"Hey."

"Fist, we need to talk about you-know-who, did you do it? Don't answer that," the voice said before Fist had a chance to say something. "Just get your arse down here. You need to get out of town anyway, you'll get some visitors from the other tribe if you don't. You've made a big fuckin' mess of this and we're not happy."

Fist had let the man ramble before he spoke.

"Look, if it's all the same to you, I'll take my leave of things and give you a big get-fucked. I'll sort myself out, no thanks to you gutless pricks."

The voice paused.

"It's not that simple Fist, you know that. We need to talk first."

"Well, I've got things to do. I'll pop in when they're done," the last bit in a sarcastic tone before he broke the connection.

The one thing he hadn't thought about was retribution from the Ferals. He didn't think that Argo had been particularly well-liked, but on reflection he thought he should still watch his back. He decided to make one last run home to grab a few things. He would come back and wait to get a look at this Craig

Lune prick, maybe smack him round a bit to see if he was involved. If it doesn't come to anything I'll just head to Newcastle.

"Before we go past my place, I want to get a gun from my brother's place. They're still away and I've still got the keys."

"Luny, is that a good idea, let's not make this worse."

"Fucked if I'm going without a fight," Luny said with finality.

Dek parked in the driveway. Luny ran inside and grabbed a gun, carry case and a box of cartridges. They drove back to Luny's, doing a slow pass up the street. There were no Harleys or vehicles with occupants.

"Be quick," was all Dek said.

Luny didn't need to be told.

Rider was annoyed with herself and very annoyed with Deklin Stephens. She hadn't anticipated the sort of response she got, figuring he would go to water. She wondered whether she was losing control and wasting potential opportunities. She began to think that she should say something to Plumber or maybe her boss but then thought better of it, convincing herself that she still didn't know anything, other than the fact that some angry bikies might be visiting Craig Lune some time soon.

Rider decided to stake out Lune's house figuring this would be the place where things might happen.

And she was right. World's collided in Luny's street.

Rider saw Lune run across the footpath to his building from a grey Honda Euro just as she parked at the top of his street. She'd only been there a few minutes when she could hear the unmistakable sound of an approaching Harley Davidson.

She saw the Harley in her mirror just as Lune ran back out of the building, carrying a backpack, and climbed into the Honda. The big bike passed her by, just as the Honda pulled out. The bike fell in behind the Honda and began to follow it. Rider fell in behind.

Dek heard the Harley just after Rider.

"Come on Luny, move it," he said out loud, willing Luny back to the car.

Luny sprinted out of the doors to his building at a rate of knots that convinced Dek that Luny had heard it too. Luny was barely in the seat before Dek accelerated down the street. He looked in his mirror to see the big bike close behind him.

"Well, at least we know where the enemy is."

Luny looked into the side mirror to confirm what Dek saw.

"At least there's only one of them. What do we do?"

"Let's just head towards Merimbula. The petrol tank is full, let's see what happens. Maybe you should load that gun."

Luny looked at Dek and shook his head.

"Who are you?"

19

Fist saw the guy run out of the building and jump into the car. He couldn't be a hundred percent sure he had the right person but, by the looks of the haste he was making, Fist figured the odds were looking okay. He decided to follow. Thankfully he'd only recently filled the tank.

At the first red light they came to, Fist ride up beside the Honda to peer into the vehicle. The two men stared at him as he did at them. He thought the guy in the passenger seat looked familiar. The guy in the driver seat smiled and pointed his index finger, simulating a gun, and pulling the trigger.

When the light turned green Fist pulled back in behind the Honda and followed from a distance.

Luny thumped Dek in the shoulder.

"What the fuck did you do that for," he demanded, more in panic than anger.

"What, you think we might make him angry?"

"Well you've fucking confirmed we're the ones he's after."

"Aw Luny, I think he already decided that."

Luny leaned between the seats and pulled the shotgun from its case on the back seat. He slid two cartridges into the barrels and clicked the gun closed. He slid the case over the top of the gun.

"Should I let him see the gun?" asked Luny.

"Nah, let's save the surprise. You'd probably have every cop within five kilometres circling around us if someone else saw it."

They drove through the city and headed for the coastal highway. The Harley stayed close behind them.

Rider sat back from the Harley pondering her next move. She was starting to feel a little nervous that things were out of her control, building to a climax that could land her in hot water. She was thinking about Plumber when he called.

"Hey, where are you?" he asked.

"Just out doing some chores."

"You sound funny, everything okay?"

"No, it's all fine."

"Can we catch up later, I was thinking about coming over."

"I'm not sure when I'll be back. I'll give you a call."

"Have you heard that someone shot the head of the Ferals? We're looking for our old mate Fist to have a chat with him."

"No, I hadn't heard that," Rider paused. "Anything to the do with our operation?"

"Ah, who the fuck knows with these secretive pricks."

"Ok, I'll talk to you later." She broke the connection, wondering whether there was a link. She hadn't thought much about which Mongrel she was following. She'd only seen a picture of Fist from the operation file and hadn't had an opportunity to see who was on the bike.

"Well, what do we do?" asked Luny. "He's not going anywhere and we don't want him following us to the house."

"Yeah. I was thinking, why don't we go through the back way that the bikies used. You can drive, you'll be able to lose him on the dirt roads. We can take another road down the mountain. He won't be able to keep up."

"How can I get into the driver's seat?"

"We'll just stop in the next town. He won't do anything. I might grab a pie."

"A fucking pie? How can you think about pies at a time like this?"

"Chill mon," Dek did a very bad Jamaican accent.

"I don't get you, this could go badly and you seem to get more relaxed. What are you on?"

"It's all good. Here, let's stop and change seats."

They had entered the small town where Luny had waited for the bikies on the day of the operation. Dek park in the same spot where Luny had stopped. The Harley stopped just up the street.

"You want anything," said Dek, sauntering across the street in the direction of the bakery, giving way to a white Subaru which pulled in and parked a bit further down the street.

"No I fucking don't."

Luny looked around at the Harley. The rider sat astride his machine with the motor running. Luny had a feeling he was one of the gang that had followed them into the camp ground and started shooting at them. But he wasn't sure.

Rider drove past the parked Harley, glancing at the rider, knowing instantly that it was, indeed, Tony Ellery, a.k.a Fist.

"Shit," she said out loud, as she parked beyond the grey Honda. She wished that Plumber hadn't told her that they were looking for Fist, now she had a real dilemma. If she didn't tell Plumber, and he found out that she had been following Fist, she was going to get in real trouble.

Just for a while, she decided, she could get a way with claiming she couldn't tell which bikie it was.

Fist was getting the shits. He couldn't believe one of the fuckers had gone into the pie shop. He was tempted to storm over and kick his arse when he came out.

But before he had a chance to action his unpleasant thoughts, the bloke strode across the road with some bags. He placed them on the roof of the car, while he opened the door. He waved at Fist and then climbed inside.

Fist just stared.

Dek had bought a steak and kidney pie and a

lamington for himself. He had also bought Luny a sausage roll.

"Just in case the aroma of these fine victuals tempt your taste buds."

Luny, stared and just shook his head as he reversed onto the highway.

The Harley followed.

When the Honda turned off the highway to the right, both Fist and Rider thought it was getting a bit weird, following the same route the bikies had taken during their failed trip to Eden to buy the pseudoephydrine.

Fist started to wonder if he was being suckered into something.

Rider had no idea whatsoever, and was nervous they would soon know she was following them.

When Luny turned onto the gravel road ten minutes later, Fist swore, knowing he would struggle to keep up if they drove fast. And drive fast they did.

As soon as Luny steered onto the gravel he moved the transmission into manual shift mode and stomped on the accelerator, the engine roared and the front drive-wheels scrabbled for purchase on the loose purchase.

They left Fist in no doubt as to their intent.

But Fist was no mug on a bike. He went as hard as

he could in their wake, slowing loosing ground as the nimble car went hard at each corner.

By the time they reached the next village, the bike had just topped the final rise for the run down almost a kilometre behind. Luny and Dek went through the village far beyond the posted speed. Neither noticed the little boy wave from the yard of the last house, where he sat on his bike.

Fist never returned the wave either as he concentrated on making up some lost ground on the sealed roads.

"Take the next left," said Dek, "it'll take us in the same direction but it's a gravel road."

Luny said nothing, totally focused on braking hard at the final moment to turn onto the gravel road. He glanced in his mirror before he turned.

"He's not that far back," said Luny, concern in his voice.

"Don't worry, this is a long and twisty road."

Dek was right. The road started down the mountain and was a continuous series of tight gravel corners with many corrugations that shook the car as Luny went as hard as he dared. He spared a quick thought for the hours he had put into his rally game on the Playstation and had a brief smirk to himself.

Dek still looked very relaxed, even though the rear of the vehicle slid out on many of the corners.

"You know we could stop this," said Dek, over the roar of the engine and the rattle of tyres over the corrugations.

"What do you mean?" said Luny, sawing the steering wheel from side to side in an effort to keep the car on the inside of the corner and away from the steep drop on the outside.

"We could just stop, over the top of one of these rises, and surprise him with the gun. We don't need to hurt him, just get him to stop and disable the bike."

Luny spared a quick glance at his companion.

"Okay, but you'll have to do it, I'll have to get the car stopped."

"Oh, I'm happy to do it," was all Dek said.

"Get the gun into the front with you, so you can get out quickly. Be fucking careful, it's loaded and ready to go."

Dek manoeuvred the long-barrelled weapon into the front seat.

"No rock-salt this time Dek, you hit him, there's a good chance you'll kill him."

Dek nodded but said nothing. Luny stood on the brakes as the topped a rise. The car stopped in a skid.

Luny pushed his door open. He could here the Harley coming along behind but some distance back.

Dek walked back up the road a little and waited.

Rider was in a bit of a panic. She wasn't used to driving fast on dirt roads, so even the Harley had started to pull away from her. By the time she passed through the small village she had lost sight of the bike and the car. She cursed and put her foot down on the sealed road, taken slightly aback at the sight of a small boy waving to her.

When she reached the turn-off that the others had taken she slowed. She could see skid marks on the gravel and what looked like a motorcycle tyre mark in the loose gravel.

The road ahead was even worse than the previous gravel section and she cursed as she had to slow for the tight corners ahead of her.

As Dek heard the Harley about to top the rise ahead of him he stepped into the middle of the road and swung the gun up to his shoulder and took aim.

When Fist saw him at the last moment, he stood on the brakes, locking the rear wheel and almost losing control of the big machine. He pulled it to a stop in a cloud of dust, not much more than a metre from where Dek stood pointing the gun at his chest.

"Please turn it off and step off."

Luny had stepped out of the car to watch. He was in awe of Dek's tone and control.

Wrestling the big machine to a stop meant that Dek had no opportunity to pull his sawn-off from its scabbard. He could've headed straight for the guy with the gun but didn't like his chances of surviving the encounter.

Fist killed the engine, kicked down the side stand and stepped off his bike.

"What now blondie," he said to Dek. "You going to kill me?" It came out, almost as a scoff. Too many guns had been pointed at Fist in the past for him to show anything close to fear.

"No, no," Dek replied in a calm, almost patronising tone. "You appear to be following us. Just going to make sure your machine can't go any further. You'll have a nice walk from here." With that Dek swung his aim back towards Fist's bike.

"Whoa, whoa," said Fist. "Hang on, just a second, lets talk about this."

"Talk about what?"

"About what I want."

"And what is it you want?"

Luny had walked up the road and was standing behind Dek.

"Some of the money you pricks stole from us."

"You really need to work on your interpersonal skills. Mr…?"

"Fist."

Dek smiled and Luny gave a small start at the name they heard over the listening device.

"Ah, Mr Fist, we've heard of you, or I should say, we heard you."

Fist looked quizzical but said nothing.

Dek continued.

"When you talked to my friend here you said you wanted all of the money, now's it's just some of it. I'm getting conflicting messages here."

"Look, I'm the only one in the club who knows it was you two. I'm a bit on the outer with them and looking to move on. Give me half, and your secret is safe with me. We can just go our separate ways."

Luny started to say something but Dek raised his hand.

"Assuming we have this money, my biggest concern is one of trust Mr Fist. You're not sending out trustworthy vibes."

"Look, I've got no love for the club, they've fucked me over, I don't give a shit about them. It's worth the risk for you, because if you don't I'm going to tell them who you are. They won't even care about getting the money back, they'll just want pay back. You'll just disappear, simple as that."

Fist's matter-of-fact description frightened both Dek and Luny. Before Dek could respond, all three turned, looking back up the mountain road, hearing an approaching vehicle. Fist smirked.

"Well Mr Blondie, what do we do now. An impasse, I believe you tossers would call it. You'd better put the gun down, we don't want the cops coming back to visit us."

Dek knew Fist was right and laid the shotgun in the rough drain on the inside of the road. Fist pushed his bike off to the opposite side of the ride. Dek and Luny were looking up the road and didn't see Fist slip the sawn-off out of its bucket and inside his jacket.

Rider wasn't travelling very fast. She had long given up on the idea she would see the bike or the car again. She had decided to call Plumber and tell him what she was doing but couldn't get phone reception.

When she topped the small rise she was shocked to see the three men standing about on the road. She stopped well short of them. She didn't know what to do. She didn't have a gun, so arresting Ellery was not an option.

The men were staring at her. One of them, it must have been Stephens, waved his arm, signalling for her to keep driving. Rider didn't want to drive past, knowing that Stephens or Lune would recognise her. She decided to turn around, she drove back up the road a short distance and stopped out of sight turning the car around again to face down the mountain, knowing she would hear the Harley start up and head off.

The three men watched the car turn around.

"She didn't much like the look of you," said Dek turning towards Fist. Dek's smile disappeared as he saw that Fist was holding a sawn-off in one hand.

"Not so funny now, smart-mouth prick."

Luny and Dek said nothing.

"Right, enough fucking about, where's the money?"

"It's obviously not here," said Luny. "We'll give you two hundred."

Dek swung around to look at him but said nothing.

"Two-fifty would make it nice and even," Fist said with a leering smile.

Dek shrugged at Luny.

"Alright, two-fifty it is. The cash is back in Canberra."

"I'm going to trust you," said Fist. He looked at his watch. "I'll call you at four pm and tell you where to bring it. You fuck me around even slightly and I'll make a call to some very unfriendly boys."

Fist slid the sawn-off back into its bucket, climbed onto the bike and headed back up the mountain. Dek and Luny followed suit.

Rider heard the Harley start. She was about to drive on down the mountain when she realised that it the sound was coming towards her not away. There was nothing she could do but keep driving. Ellery stared straight at her as he passed but kept going. Rider stopped on the side of the road.

She waited until he was out of sight around the next bend before turning around to follow. Rider decided to ignore the men in the car and follow Ellery until she had phone range, when she would call Plumber.

She started to think about her story and why it had taken so long to call him.

Dek picked up the shotgun and they both climbed back into the car.

"Well, that could've been worse," he said.

"My head is spinning. I feel like we totally lost control." Luny was rattled.

"Look, we're okay. Short of killing him, we don't have an option. We have to trust him. All things being equal we'll still have a nice stash, and be free and clear to enjoy it."

"This new-found wisdom of your is truly troubling."

Luny turned the car around, heading back up the mountain road at a much more pedestrian pace than he had driven down.

When Rider slowed for the tight turn onto a small bridge, her heart jumped into her mouth as Ellery stepped into the middle of the road, the sawn off pointed straight at her.

She put her foot down and drove straight at him. He jumped aside and fired at the car, the windscreen splintering into a spider web of cracks but remained largely intact. Pellets passed through into the passenger side, burying in the passenger seat.

In her effort to run Ellery over, Rider's car was caught in the loose gravel on the edge of the road. The wheels spun and the car slipped further off the road, the outside wheels dropping into a gutter cut deep and ragged by heavy rain. Her car came to a grinding halt.

"Get the fuck out of your car bitch," Fist yelled, as he ran up to Rider's window. "Who the fuck are you? Give me your wallet."

She did as she was bid.

"A cop from Canberra, what the fuck do you want?"

"I was following the two blokes in the car," she lied.

"Then why the fuck were you following me and why try to run me over?"

"You pointed a gun at me."

She saw the slight doubt in his eyes.

"Look, put the gun down. Don't make it worse. It's a misunderstanding, we can sort this out."

Before he could respond, Dek and Luny drove up the road and stopped beside Fist.

"Do you know who this is," said Fist, "she said she was following you."

"Yes. She's a Canberra cop. She told us you were after us. Something about a drug operation."

"Well it's pretty obvious she knows we're connected now," snarled Fist.

"No, no," Dek implored. "She doesn't know anything. Think about it. She's a constable. No-one else has been involved. If there was some evidence of anything, they wouldn't be sending a female constable. She's just a bit nosy. Let's just leave her before this gets any worse."

"No chance, she knows something." Fist turned back pointing the gun into Rider's face. "Talk to me sweetheart, what do you know?"

Rider was shaking.

"Like that guy said, I'm just a bit nosy. I was following them because I thought they were involved in something. It's nothing to do with you. I'm sorry this happened. It was my fault. I'll sort it out."

Fist laughed.

"You'll sort it out. Fuckin' funny. I'll do the sorting. He turned back towards the car. You two fuck off and leave this with me."

"Can't do that, I'm afraid," said Dek, his tone very even. Luny looked down to where he could see Dek's hands settling on the stock of the shot gun which was beside him, the barrel pointed towards Dek's feet.

"Let's just leave the young woman be, she doesn't know anything."

Fist waved the barrel of the sawn-off.

"Fuck off now, or it'll get worse for you as well."

"Sorry old son," said Dek, swinging the barrel of the gun up from his feet. Fist realised what he was doing and started to bring his own weapon to bear on Dek. It was awkward for Dek, he had to make sure the barrel came out cleanly, and didn't connect with the dash and the window frame. Fist's route was much simpler and shorter.

Both guns boomed together. The noise inside the car had the effect of a concussion grenade.

Rider had dived down beside her car, worried that Dek's shot might hit her. She didn't know who had been hit.

Luny had ducked as well. Fearing that Fist would hit the both of them.

Luny looked up, expecting the worst. He couldn't see Fist. Apart from the ringing in his ears, it was very quiet. Dek was sitting, twisted towards the door, like a statue, looking out the window, still holding the gun. A tendril of smoke came from the end of the barrel.

Luny couldn't see if he was wounded and was afraid to ask.

"Dek," he said in a gentle tone, "are you ok?"

Dek turned towards him, a grin on his face.

"That was fucking surreal."

"Are you hit?"

"Nah, nah. Good as gold. Can't say the same for old Fisty cuffs out there."

Both men got out of the car. Fist was lying in the ditch. The shot had taken him in the face. Neither man would have been able to recognise him if they had just happened upon the scene. Rider came out from behind her car to stare down at Fist.

After a time, Luny broke the silence.

"What happens now?"

Both men looked towards Rider.

Rider continued to stare at Fist.

20

Rider slept most of the next day, feeling much better when she finally rose from her bed. She went back to work on Monday, waiting for news about Fist's demise. It didn't take long.

Plumber called her on Monday afternoon and said Fist's body had been found, oddly, not that far where the drug operation had gone wrong. He asked whether he could come over that night. Rider said no, deciding that she would tell him it was over.

She spent most of the day thinking about what had transpired, thinking about the two men, and about what she needed to do.

Dek had driven Rider home.

Rider had been all business when they had dragged

Fist's body and his Harley into the bush but by the time they had helped her to push her car back onto the road, the shock of what had almost transpired, settled on her like a blanket.

It was obvious to the two men, she looked pale and a bit wobbly on her feet.

After pushing out the broken windscreen, Dek insisted that he drive her home in his car. Rider was grateful. Luny wasn't overjoyed with the arrangement. He was left to the breezy drive in Rider's car and he didn't feel much better than Rider.

When they had dropped Rider and her car off at her flat, Dek drove Luny home.

Luny eventually broke the silence.

"Are you okay?" Luny asked, "you know, about what happened and what you had to do."

Dek took a moment before he responded. He had stopped at a red light and turned to look at Luny.

"It's weird, and maybe it'll change, but the only thing that bothers me, is that it doesn't bother me. It needed doing, I did it. Bizarre. I didn't enjoy it, but it certainly wasn't hard to do. A bit scary really."

Dek laughed. "Maybe it's my calling Luny. I could be a hit man."

Luny stared at his friend, open-mouthed.

"Kidding Luny, lighten up."

"What do you think Rider will do? What did she say to you on the way home?"

Rider had said little during the drive and had eventually fallen asleep, waking as they drove into Canberra. She had waited until they were almost back at her flat before touching Dek's arm and saying a simple thank-you.

21

Two men and an attractive woman sat down to brunch at an outside table on a brisk Canberra Saturday morning. Privacy was more important than warmth.

They ordered coffees, saying nothing further until the waiter was well away. Rider spoke first.

"Well, as I suspected, Ellery's death was put down to retribution from the Ferals. They're following up on that, but doubtful they'll get anywhere."

Dek and Luny both exhaled in relief. Rider looked into Dek's eyes.

"Thanks, again."

Dek smiled.

"You're welcome."

Rider continued.

"Now, before you tell me your tale I wanted to say something. I suspect you're wondering a bit about what I did or didn't do, being a cop and all," she paused to look both men in the eyes.

"The bottom line is, I cocked up. I shouldn't have taken things as far as I did. I'd never say this to anyone but you two, but I can be a bit over-zealous. I really wanted to nail someone over the drug operation. It kind of took over and I lost a bit of perspective. I can assure you I won't be telling anyone about what happened. I'd be in as much trouble as you two. Probably more trouble. You two still haven't really broken any laws."

"Dek would probably get a medal for shooting that filth, Ellery, and saving a cop." Rider smiled at Dek, again. "So don't be concerned."

"Now," said Rider, leaning back in her chair, "as you promised, I want the fully story."

Dek and Luny explained how they had bugged the clubhouse, and the subsequent operation to relieve the Mongrels of their cash.

Rider stopped them at the appropriate time, explaining what had happened to her. Both men were shocked to learn what had gone on in their wake, but not as shocked as Rider, when she learned what had transpired at the campground in the bush.

When the breakfast arrived the conversation stopped until after second coffees were taken.

Rider asked why they did it.

The two men looked at each other.

"I'm not really sure." Luny answered first. "It was his idea. I think we were just bored. I never really thought we would get to the point that we would do anything. It just kind of crept up on me in stages."

Dek laughed.

"I definitely needed this more than Luny," his eyes twinkled. "The problem is, I think I've got a taste for it, not the shooting stuff, just the adrenalin."

Luny looked at his friend.

"Don't even think about it!"

The three of them laughed. Rider's next question cut through the laughter.

"So, how much?"

Luny and Dek looked at each other. This was the part they had been dreading. They'd discussed it at length during the week following Fist's death.

Given that Rider had helped them to pull Fist's body off the road and push his Harley into the bush, they were confident that they wouldn't be in any sort of police trouble.

But what concerned them, was that if Rider wasn't going to tell anyone in the police about what had happened then she must be angling for a slice of the cash. They were in a similar position to what they found themselves in with Fist. Both agreed it would be worth giving up the two-fifty that Fist had wanted to ensure that Rider was a part of the crime.

So when Rider asked 'how much', Luny said, "we thought, two-fifty."

"What do you mean 'we thought'. You must know how much you got. Two-fifty isn't much," she said. "Hardly worth it for that."

Luny looked at Dek.

"No, we got more than that, that's how much we're offering you," said Dek.

Rider's face went blank and then she laughed. Her face lit up.

"I wasn't after your money, I was just curious."

"Sorry, we just figured you'd want a slice," said Luny.

"What, and you were just going to give me two-hundred-and-fifty-thousand dollars for no reason, on top of saving my life? You blokes aren't really hard-core criminals are you?"

All three of them laughed.

"So how much?"

"Seven-fifty," said Luny.

"That's better, almost makes it worth it," said Rider.

"I do have one request," Rider paused for effect, turning to Dek, "how about you buy me an expensive dinner."

Printed in Australia
AUHW011841220622
365345AU00026B/740

9 780648 421504